Praise for
PRIOR CONVICTIONS
and LIA MATERA

"The author writes with intelligence and feeling about issues that still hurt and people who still care."

The New York Times Book Review

"Blessed with pungent prose, an affecting, funny, realistic heroine/detective and pressing moral and emotional issues."

San Francisco Chronicle

"Matera's wit, grace with language, irreverence toward the legal system, and wry dissection of being a child of the children of the Sixties make this a standout work. . . . If you want to catch an author on the verge of bestsellerdom, read this."

The Kirkus Reviews

"Readers will be shaken by Matera's rapier-sharp dissection of personal relationships and radical ideologies. Matera again demonstrates that she is one of today's best mystery writers."

Publishers Weekly

LM

PRIOR CONVICTIONS

Lia Matera

BALLANTINE BOOKS • NEW YORK

Library of Congress Catalog Card Number: 90-25203

ISBN 0-345-37445-2

This edition published by arrangement with Simon & Schuster, Inc.

Manufactured in the United States of America

First Ballantine Books Edition: May 1992

To Kevin Lewis and Sherri Paris—
For support and hilarity
in a time of personal and geologic
earthquakes.

The best lack all conviction, while the worst are full of passionate intensity.

—William Butler Yeats, "The Second Coming"

PROLOGUE

Tom Tom Tom. Walking in step, Tom Tom Tom after all these years. Tom with his crazy sister and his squat brown mother. Tom a body that looked best damp, a bicep, a tone of voice. A beast of hair and muscle. *Bestia*, his mother called him. Tense in clothes, straining at the seams. I remember him at antiwar rallies, his huge torso heaving with the violence of his emotions. Tomasino Rugieri, after all these years, what will prison have done to you?

Or maybe what we hear about prisons is a myth, an exaggeration to keep us straight. I've often wondered, often hoped so. We certainly didn't let it stop us then. "They're gonna bust all our asses soon enough," the boy on the makeshift platform would shout, and the crowd would cheer him even before he added, "Why not make it April seventeenth," or December 18, or whenever the next demonstration would be.

I tried not to be afraid of jail, but I was. I was also afraid of National Guardsmen that ringed our Boston College rallies, afraid of riot-geared police that spilled from convoys of trucks. I didn't stay away, but I kept to the back of the crowd. I stayed where I could turn and run, safe and anonymous. If Nixon hadn't been burning peasant children in Vietnam, I'd have skipped it. I was all paranoid eyes, scanning, watching. Other people focused on the speaker, on the chanting. I admired the anger on their faces.

But then, hardly any of us went to jail. Some conscientious objectors, the unlucky ones with the low numbers. The ones that hadn't found that blend of Jesus and Gandhi that convinces draft boards, the ones that couldn't write pacific essays.

Tom wouldn't write an essay. "This is the only essay the draft board gets from me, Christine," he announced, weighing a brick in his big square hand.

His mother flew into a rage when she heard him say that. She laced her fingers through his thick black curls and pulled until he clamped his hand around her heavy wrist. "*Bestia*," beast, I'll hear her scream until the day I die. Then she curled the fingers of her other hand into a ball and hammered on his chest, his face. "You trying to kill me, *bestia*," she howled.

"I don't write essays for fascists," he shouted back. He caught her other wrist, forced her to stand back, frowned at her until she snapped both wrists clear and wrapped her short arms around his neck. And sobbed.

His sister Irene burst through the kitchen door, her thick black brows drawn together in outrage, her lips pulled away from her teeth. "Leave her alone!" she shrieked. "You're an animal!"

And me, my heart racing, watching the contours of that animal body under strained clothing. Tom a thick lawn of body hair, a massive rib cage under my greedy fingers.

His collective disapproved of me. They accused Tom of "waning commitment." They said he'd built a wall around us and forgotten the work that had to be done. He got furious and said he was entitled to a personal relationship. They said maybe if the relationship were an equal partnership with an "aware and liberated individual dedicated to the struggle."

Tom leaped out of his chair when they said that. "My personal life is private—it is not policy, it is not strategy, it is not open to discussion." There was a long silence, and someone pulled out a copy of the Weather Underground's *Prairie Fire*. Tom knocked it out of her hand. There's a part in it about smashing monogamy because it holds up the corporate structure.

Someone else said, "You can see he's got Chris up on a pedestal."

I gathered up my stuff and left. Tom followed me. That night he moved me out of the dorms and into his apartment. That might have been the night I got pregnant; my pills were packed away somewhere.

I would have married Tom anyway. His mother Santina's heart was broken by our living together. And somehow, her heart was important to me, a fragile bloom on an old prickly pear. More important to me than my own mother's feelings. My parents, I knew, would threaten to disown me, the suburbanites' meager arsenal. But to me, my mother was a cold, powdered cheek, father's slender socialite. Santina was special, vibrant, extravagantly, unapologetically foreign. The ferocity of her embrace when I told her I would become Tom's wife, the way she said, "I know you no was one of those cheap *puttane*," it added something to my small store of self-worth.

When my friends found out I'd gotten married, they were disgusted. "Why?" was the common reaction. Even people without political objections to monogamy found it limiting and inconvenient.

But I could see it made a difference to Tom to be married. I wasn't sure what difference or why, but on our wedding day there was pride, or something, in his eyes. Just like Santina, alternately weeping onto my neck, her coarse hair rough against my chin, and toasting me with anisetto, her cheeks flushed above a gap-toothed smile.

After that, Santina counseled me continually. She'd thought of a dozen ways to save Tom, but believed that as his wife I had the superior claim to impose my will on him. "You tell him go to Canada, he listen to you" was her favorite fantasy. And law school. "Luigi the grocer boy he go and they no did draft him."

Four of her brothers had died in the Second World War. One died in Greece, one died in a German prisoner-of-war camp, another, a partisan, had been shot "like a bandit" by the Americans, and the youngest, too young to be drafted, had been blown to pieces racing across a piazza while his sisters looked on from the balcony of their city apartment.

"I never forget," Santina told me more than once. "I look up and see the American plane. Next thing Francuccio and all a Piazza Giulia is a big boom and fire and dust. Oh, the dust." She'd cover half her olive face with a fat ringless hand. "The next day we hear from a *compare* that the *maledetti* Germans they get my brother Gigetto."

She went to Mass every morning to ask God what had made her oldest brother become a partisan, why he'd given the fascists an excuse to burn down the family's house in the village. "If we no had to go from Terra Spaccata to *la città*, Francuccio he would be here in America with me today— maybe a big shot." And she'd conclude her story as she concluded all her stories, by wiping away tears and dragging her wooden spoon along the sides of the big pot of spaghetti sauce perennially bubbling on the stove.

When Tom's lottery number came up sixteen, I begged him to see a lawyer. "I haven't done anything wrong and I *don't need a goddam apologist, sellout fucking lawyer*." His black eyes glittered warning: end of discussion.

I went to consciousness-raising sessions with women friends, but their problems seemed trivial compared to Tom's; sex roles didn't land you in prison, or at least I didn't think so until I had children. The women looked down on me for talking about Tom so much.

I waited for the government to indict my husband.

And while I waited, I met a man. In an Italian literature course I'd taken to please Santina, though she had no interest whatever in my studies, and was illiterate herself.

His name was Edward Hershey. He was tall and slim, long-legged, with a serious face and green eyes. He was very male, but softer than Tom, kinder maybe, certainly more yielding. One day he was a friend, the next day he was my lover. I think I loved Tom for his body, our bodies, for the animal connection I felt to him. I loved his fire, his foreignness, how different he was from me. But I understood Edward; he was like me, mayonnaise on white bread and fighting it. He was easy to talk to; we could rely on common references and emotional shorthand. For a few amazing weeks, I made love to both of them.

That was twenty years ago. I was celibate a long time after that.

When Tom found out about me and Edward, he went berserk and broke my arm. I guess he'd been suspicious for a while. Sometimes he'd insist I stay in. He'd pin me to the wall with his big body. "We're at meetings every fucking night. As long as we're home, let's act married."

The night he found out about Edward, I'd gotten carried away. Kissing Edward under a streetlight, I heard myself say, I love you. It scared me, scared Edward, too, I think; he didn't reply in kind.

Maybe someone saw us walking across campus together. Maybe Tom saw us. He wasn't at his collective, like I thought he was. He was home before me. Before I climbed the last flight to what we called our "cottage," he opened the door.

I felt unsteady, a tight, mindless flutter, pure apprehension. I tried to find something in that small tenement apartment, something I could do to keep from fidgeting.

Tom grabbed my wrist, jerking my arm till I heard the bone snap.

My God, it hurt. The fear choked me and froze me in place, like in a nightmare. I was looking up at Tom, shielding myself with my other arm, trying to protect myself, crushed under the hatred in his eyes, watching the tears stream down his contorted face, watching his huge arm pull back and snap forward like a spring. I was so shocked I couldn't scream, couldn't push a sound through my trachea.

Tom said something in Italian. Italian!

Santina told me once about the dressmaker in her village. Her husband had gone to Germany to work, like so many other unemployed southern Italians. The dressmaker was young and beautiful by village standards and, as the lonely years went by, she took a lover. And somebody, a villager passing through Germany, told her husband. The husband immediately hopped on a train. He sneaked back into the village in the dead of night and disfigured his wife with a straight razor while the entire village listened to her screams of agony and terror. Then he disrobed her and marched her from house to house denouncing her as an adulteress.

"For days his mamma she keep a calling everybody to her house and say, 'Come and see the *puttana*,' and her, *poverella*, on a bed *nuda* crying, her face and chest . . ." Santina implied the slash marks with her finger. The husband searched for his wife's lover for days to kill him, but the lover had jumped a boat to America. The husband went back to Germany and never sent his wife another penny. "She did go become a *prostituta* in Roma," Santina continued gravely, "for the *porchi Americani*." Family honor, she explained. The husband had no choice.

I'd always thought of Tom as an American with an Italian mother. I was wrong.

Tom wouldn't speak to me after that. I heard our women friends hassled him, heckled him at meetings. He stopped going. By the time I was able to search for him, he'd dropped out of sight. I was desperate for him, spent all my money on detectives, newspaper ads. I was four months pregnant by then, wider but not really showing.

His mother slammed the door in my face. "*Puttana*," whore, was all she'd say, "no divorce!" She left me standing there crying, my arm encased in plaster, wondering how, after all the stories over pasta, all the agonizing over Tom's future, she could think I'd come to ask for a divorce.

Tom's sister dashed out after me. Her heavy-featured face was flushed. She looked angry, as always. I thought she meant to spit at me and I cringed. Instead she put her arms around me and said the most terrible things about Tom that I have ever heard anyone say about another person. I backed out of her arms. Her embrace had hurt me. She was squinting, sneering. I felt nauseous. She told me Tom had joined Highway 61, a radical group that every once in a while sent someone from its Boston headquarters to our rallies to urge us to bomb factories.

I ran out of money. I stayed with my parents, who took one look at my arm and speculated that I'd brought it on myself. ''Not one of us''—that was their assessment of Tom. One of us would never do something like that. They'd sit in front of their television watching footage of Vietnamese villages in flames and tell me Mediterranean people were violent by nature. In softer moments, my mother supposed her brother the California lawyer might help Tom beat his draft indictment. *If* Tom was civilized about the divorce.

I kept my mouth shut because they weren't worth arguing with. Nor did I have the energy. I did what I was used to doing: I coexisted with them. Maybe that's my pattern; I did it later with my second husband. Only with Tom did I stretch and struggle.

I got in touch with Highway 61 (from a Bob Dylan song where God tells Abraham to kill his son, and says to do it on Highway 61). I didn't say I was looking for Tom, and I gave my mother's maiden name so he wouldn't blackball me if he heard I'd called. It was two months before they trusted me enough to let me meet with anyone important. I helped them any way I could, hoping I'd see Tom. I made coffee. I made booby traps. I made myself believe in it. Living with my parents made class hatred easy.

Then I made the biggest mistake of my life.

I told one of the Highwaypeople that my parents were leaving for Europe, that I'd have their nice big house to my-self all summer.

If, on the Fourth of July, I hadn't gone into labor so strained and intense that home birth ceased to be an option, I'd have ended up a prisoner in that house. The other prisoner in the house, an innocent baby (not mine), would probably have been murdered. And my husband Tom might not have gone to prison after all.

1

I WATCHED MY marijuana float away from the Santa Monica pier. At the last minute, an eddy of gray water sent it swirling back toward me. It seemed to call out, *Willa, no; I'm your last vestige of hipness*. I almost jumped into the water to reclaim the damp detritus of my one remaining vice. My one remaining vice—God, I'd gotten boring.

But I thought of all the mornings I'd wakened feeling like a bad country-western song. Every morning for the last year. And many mornings for many years before that. I'd been smoking pot since I was thirteen, in fact; since a cute boy with an earring handed me a joint on Haight Street, near my parents' flat. I had enough undamaged left brain to realize (if not exactly comprehend) that that was almost twenty-five years ago. I'd accomplished a lot in spite of it—and in spite of the nomadic movement politics that defined the life-style. A decade later than most of my peers, I'd endured Stanford University, Malhousie Law School, and two legal associate jobs—one politically correct, one fiscally correct. Maybe I'd needed pot to help me put up with the bullshit. But it worried me that I now needed it every single day.

Anyway, I reminded myself, this was a good time to quit. I was embarking on a (slightly premature) midlife crisis. I'd just left the best job—rather, the best income—I'd ever had. My sex life was lying somewhere with a wooden stake in its heart. My mood was beyond repair; I might as well give my brain cells a chance to regenerate.

Behind me on the pier, an Iranian couple noisily unfolded a quilted-steel hot dog wagon. Early rollerbladers strapped on knee pads. A Vietnamese man with an armload of buckets baited fish hooks. I shook the last few flakes of pot out of my Baggie and watched them sift through a layer of yellow smog. Then, more discreetly, I dropped the Baggie off the pier. In Santa Monica, I could get more jail time for littering than for possession of a controlled substance.

I walked the length of the pier, brushing the last of the green dust off my fingers. Santa Monica, the Miami Beach of sold-out activists; fitting that I should dump my pot here. I was a straight person now, dull and unhip in the uniform of my outmoded youth: faded jeans, moccasins and a tie-dyed T-shirt. (At least my hair wasn't still long and center-parted. It was shoulder length and side-parted, the only style that looks vaguely adult on a five-one blonde who won't wear makeup and hates high heels.)

Smoking pot in grumpy solitude had been my alternative to sushi bars and health clubs with lawyers I saw enough of at work. Pot was my own little party, the last flicker of an old light show. Without it, I would probably devolve into

Marilyn Quayle. (At least the uniform of *my* youth didn't include hats that looked like dog dishes.)

I took a last, unfond look at the motels and bungalow restaurants of Santa Monica Boulevard. Then I climbed into my car, a hatchback filled with all my worldly possessions, mostly plastic hanging bags of clothes. A year at a top-dollar L.A. law firm had done wonders for my wardrobe. A few more months and I'd have been the best-dressed lawyer at the Betty Ford Clinic.

I started the car, feeling clammy and nervous. I'd lived most of my life in San Francisco, where you can get anywhere by bus, streetcar or subway. I'd never learned to drive. But by the time I'd subsidized a fleet of L.A. cabs, I decided I was flexible enough to learn. Today, I had hundreds of miles to drive before nightfall.

I was finally leaving. I'd made 346 chalk marks on the walls of my Westwood apartment (stucco, of course; wall-to-wall carpeting; utterly characterless and bland, as I was fast becoming). I'd served my time. My résumé had been paroled.

Leaving was the good news. The bad news would fill several volumes.

Yes, I'd rehabilitated my résumé. It had taken a year of squinting at loan agreements and conferring with obnoxious men in red power ties, but I'd done it. I was now marketable—a fourth-year attorney with family law and corporate litigation experience; experienced enough to be of use but not senior enough to threaten associates on the brink of partnership. I'd have no trouble finding a job in another firm.

Unfortunately, I hated being a lawyer.

And yes, I was going home to San Francisco. I loved the city; missed it like hell; fretted myself into a tizzy when the earthquake hit and I wasn't there to panic and get in everybody's way. I should have been anxious to return. But I hadn't settled things with my parents, the original bleeding-heart activists. (My earliest childhood fantasy was not my name on a Broadway marquee. It was "Free Willa Jansson" on a mimeographed flyer.) My parents were still mad at me for taking a socially useless (at best) job. I was still mad at them for being mad at me.

I was also fighting a stupid feeling that might have passed for love if its object had ever given me a chance to express it. But I hadn't heard from Don Surgelato the entire year I'd been in L.A.

And when, in desperation, I'd found a brilliant young therapist to help me with my problems, I'd clowned things up by falling for him, too.

So I was on my way back to San Francisco, but I didn't really want to get there. I was finally marketable, but I didn't want a job in my field. And I was turning into Marilyn Quayle.

My therapist (from whom I'd concealed my adolescent crush) thought I should stay in L.A., stay with the law firm of Wailes, Roth, Fotheringham & Beck until I got a handle on my other problems.

Instead, I accepted an unexpected job offer. As of a week from Monday, I'd be clerking for the Honorable Michael J. Shanna, federal court judge, Northern District of California.

Clerkships are usually reserved for baby Republicans fresh out of law school. I'd applied for and talked my way into this one at the urging of an old friend and former employer. I'd done it because clerkships only last a year. Any firm I joined now would want a career-long commitment, and I couldn't do that. I wasn't sure I had even a year of discipline left in me. I wasn't sure I could stand even a low-key year of writing bench memos for a judge. But it was a respectably finite job with some résumé value, and it was an excuse to leave L.A. I grabbed it.

My therapist seemed troubled, in his pointedly non-judgmental way. I pictured him in his rattan chair, looking oh-so-Manhattan—laser beam eyes, tousled hair, double-breasted suit, wire-frame glasses. (I supposed all his female patients were in love with him; I supposed it was a cliché of modern neurosis.) He suggested I "let go of the idea" of making career or life decisions now. He suggested I "float a while longer"—avoid making even the right changes for the wrong reasons.

And maybe he was right; maybe I should have stayed in L.A. Whatever else was wrong with the place, there was somebody there willing (for eighty-five dollars an hour) to listen to my problems without comparing them to those of third-world mothers.

But I never seem to take the advice of people I respect. I take my own, instead.

So I drove up the coast highway, oblivious to crashing waves, kiting pelicans, cliffs painted in ice plant. The price of admission to a midlife crisis is that you stop noticing anything that won't sleep with you.

2

I WAS RUNNING late, so I drove directly to my parents' flat. My father had phoned that morning to ask me to dinner. He said he wanted to try out a new recipe called Buddha's Feast. I said sure, I'd bring the barbecue sauce.

I climbed out of my car feeling like a clenched fist. In nine hours, my back had never touched the seat. I don't know what keeps my car on the road, and until I find out, I'm assuming it's the force of my grip on the wheel.

My parents live on a block that looks like a retrospective of urban housing trends—everything from domes and turrets to flat, unornamented plaster. The jumble of shared-wall styles made an Emerald City silhouette against a moonlit sky. I stood there a minute, drinking it in, glad to be back.

The evening air was crisp, blessedly free of the slight,

ever-present humidity of L.A. haze. I could smell black bean sauce and garlic coming from my parents' flat. My father believes spices can improve the flavor of tofu; and probably they could, if tofu had a flavor.

"Willa Jansson."

Oh, God. I tried not to recognize the voice. It couldn't be. Fate could not be so capricious and malign. (In fact, fate had nothing to do with it.)

But there he stood, ten yards from my parents' porch steps, arm outstretched. Edward Hershey, in leather jacket and Frye boots, six-feet-two of painful memories.

"What are you doing here?" he marveled.

"My parents." I waved at a narrow Victorian, in need of paint. "What are you doing here?"

"Visiting someone." He stood in arrested motion: portrait of a man under a streetlamp. Behind him, ornamented cornices caught the light like a picture frame. "You're back in the city now?"

How did he know I'd been gone?

"I start clerking for Judge Shanna next Monday. Federal court."

It was a few seconds before Edward spoke. Giving me a chance to appreciate his clipped curls and broad shoulders? "Willa, have you ever wished for something and had it, bam, happen?"

"You wished you'd run into me on a dark street?" I thought of all the years I'd wanted to use his zipper for target practice.

"I wished I knew a lawyer who owed me a favor."

"Owed you a favor?" I didn't have to add, you son of a bitch.

Two years ago I learned Edward Hershey was a detective and I asked him to trace some letters for me. He'd done a good job; big deal. Balance that against twenty years of hating him for screwing up my love life. No way I owed him anything but another punch in the nose. (I hadn't reacted well to the news that he'd given me a virus then considered more repellent than leprosy.)

He grinned. "You look great. Really fantastic."

I looked like I'd spent a lovesick year working seventy hours a week and smoking too much pot the rest of the time. My skin was so white you could see veins in my arms and blue capillaries under my eyes; I looked like an axolotl. But I was thin and I was blond; that's all Hershey ever cared about.

Hershey and a lot of other jokers. I have yet to think of a way to make my face look cranky and disparaging. And I get so tired of people being unpleasantly surprised.

Anyway, if Hershey was waiting for me to return the compliment, it was too bad. Of course he looked good—what else was new? But he wasn't going to hear it from me. He'd heard enough of my rhapsodizing in 1970.

In 1970, straight out of alternative high school, I journeyed to Boston with the blithe intention of reshaping it into a socialist city-state. Which shows how naïve I was when Edward Hershey strolled into the Peace-Action House (also known as a roach-infested Cambridge apartment), where I draft counseled.

"Why do you need a lawyer who owes you a favor? Not," I emphasized, "that I am she."

"I am she," he repeated. "You educated thing."

Hershey stepped closer, remembered the streetlamp, then stepped back into the pool of light. He looked at me as though I mattered to him. Since I knew I didn't, I was finally safe from the look. "How ya been, Willa? I've been thinking about you a lot lately."

How gratifying—I thought it, didn't say it. A year of conferring with obnoxious men in red power ties had trained me in the art of silent sarcasm.

"What have you been thinking?"

He favored me with his patented sexy squint, making me regret the question.

Making me regret a lot of things.

Edward Hershey strolled into my life at the height of the sexual revolution. The prevailing theory then was, sex feels great and it's antierotic to fuss about the person attached to the part that is pleasuring you. But as with most theories, few subscribers were purists. Most people continued, if clandestinely, to maintain minimum standards. My standards were higher than most. I refused to sleep with anyone corny. In the era of *Games People Play* and *Jonathan Livingston Seagull*, this was as devastating to my sex life as the virus I later acquired from Hershey.

But I will say this about him, he was never corny. Be careful what you wish for.

He positioned himself more carefully, allowing the streetlamp to bathe his face in light. Square, craggy, thick brows and mustache; Tom Selleck's ugly brother.

"Just wondering if you got that mess cleared up."

The San Francisco branch of Wailes, Roth, Fotheringham & Beck had disintegrated. Three lawyers quit, two died, one went to prison. That left only me.

"I went down to L.A., to the L.A. office. I was there a year. I had to stay a year for my résumé." I pressed closer to my car. Three hundred and forty-six chalk marks on the wall; I remembered how it felt when there were only six, sixty, a hundred.

"So where you staying now? Around here?"

"I sublet my old place. My tenant was supposed to be out yesterday."

"So you just got back?"

"Just now." I gestured at my hatchback.

"This really is kismet!" Edward reached out, giving my arm a squeeze. "Running into you. I can't get over it."

"Edward!" I jerked my arm away. I'd be his kismet only if I held a butcher knife and he fell on it.

"I know someone who's in trouble, who needs a lawyer desperately, not a Santa Cruz lawyer—I'm still down in S'Cruz—it can't be a local person, and it's got to be someone I can trust."

I had to laugh. Edward Hershey thinking he could trust me.

Eight months after I met Edward, I left Boston. I left to attend a trial in San Francisco—my parents' trial. They were looking at four to ten years for destruction of government property (draft files, as I recall).

The day I got home, I took part in a demonstration at the Presidio. I was arrested. I hired my parents' lawyer, Julian Warneke, to represent me.

My parents walked away with no jail time. I got two nightmarish months in the San Bruno jail.

I wrote to Edward, begging him to come west.

When he arrived, I was just out of jail, still crying for no reason and waking up in a cold sweat.

Hershey knew he'd contracted herpes, but he (says he) thought it was inactive. He didn't want to spoil our romantic reunion.

I punched him as hard as I could when I found out. I made a big, ugly scene in Washington Square near Peter and Paul's Cathedral. I like to think I'd have killed him if a nun hadn't intervened.

When I saw him years later at Julian Warneke's wake, I was still furious.

My mother had been entreating me for years to "let go of my anger." She's big on letting go of anger unless it's directed at your government.

And I did eventually let go of enough anger to have Hershey trace some letters for me. I'd let go of enough anger to stand here now and pose no threat to him.

But do him a favor?

I was about to say, "Fat fucking chance," when a squeaky voice called out, "Willa! And Edward Hershey—my goodness! How nice!"

3

MOTHER WORE HER only silk blouse, a red one with puckered seams that a grateful Salvadoran woman had sewn for her. It brought out the rosiness of her cheeks and set off the pale yellow-gray of her hair. She wore it with a Guatemalan skirt of parading brown women carrying urns and parcels. She sat along an archipelago of floor cushions, legs crossed under her skirt so that she seemed ringed by Lilliputians.

My father sat beside her wearing an ancient apron I'd decaled with the motto "Love Tofu—Don't Eat It." He looked wispy, colorless, thin; made me feel parental, made me want to force-feed him pork. His face pleated into a grin whenever our eyes met.

Behind them, a jumble of tacked-up posters, announcements and paper icons suggested the wall of a bus stop. I scanned them, noticing their focus had shifted from saving El Salvador and Nicaragua to feeding San Francisco's homeless and bleaching addicts' needles.

I sat on one end of a cushionless slingback sofa, as far from Edward Hershey as I could. I didn't want to share the couch with him. I didn't want to share my parents, my reunion or even my airspace. Damn him. Damn Mother for inviting him in.

In the room's one comfortable chair was Clement Kerrey, family friend and one of my few surviving employers. Right out of law school, I'd worked for Clement and his law partner Julian Warneke. Now Clement taught at my alma mater, Malhousie. It was Clement who'd put me in touch with Judge Shanna—partly so I could return to the city, partly so I could reachieve political correctness.

I hadn't seen him in a year and a half, so I was startled by his appearance. His steel-gray hair and clipped beard were streaked with white. Lines of tension had been erased from his forehead, and his eyes had lost their manic glitter. There was a fluorescent-light paleness to his skin, a stoop to his posture. He no longer looked like an endlessly energetic labor lawyer rushing to enjoin unfair labor practices. He looked like an aging law professor with plenty of time to read his bluebooks. Which was, I realized, exactly what he'd become.

It made me wonder about my closetful of new suits and my tidy new haircut: Did I look like just another yuppie lawyer?

There were rows of matted photographs on the wall behind him, artistic black-and-whites of working people—gifts from Clement, photos he'd taken of his clients.

He broke the ice. "What a treat! To see old friends again. What a lot of good memories." Bad ones, too, if he'd been the type to dwell on them.-"I was just talking about you today, Willa. To Harry Prough, that old rascal."

Harry Prough, left-wing lawyer titan, jailed almost four years for contempt of court after defending the radical group Highway 61.

"Talking about me?" I'd followed Prough's career with interest. I'd lived in Boston during the Highway 61 trial, though I never made it to the courthouse early enough to get a seat. I'd been thrilled to meet him years later at Julian Warneke's house, but I doubted he remembered me.

"Mmm." Clement grinned, some of the glitter back in his eyes. "He's arguing a motion before Mike Shanna next week. I told him to look for you."

From the corner of my eye, I saw Mother jerk back, her pale hand fluttering to her lips. My father took the hand firmly in his own and brought it back down to the cushion.

"Highway Sixty-one," he murmured. "Interesting case."

"Idiots. We all were." I was a little surprised to hear myself say so; wasn't even sure what I meant by it.

"The movement, you mean? To be seduced by the general militarism of the era?" Clement leaned forward, wrapping his arms around a thin knee.

Edward Hershey spoke for me, damn him. "To accept the Right's view of reality. They mow us down with tear gas and batons—"

"They did worse than that," Mother chimed in. "Look at Chicago, Kent State."

"So we figure we've got a war on our hands. The fucking war at home. The fucking revolution." Hershey sounded as cynical as I am, which momentarily endeared him to me.

Before I could speak for myself (assuming I knew what I meant to say), Clement shook his head vehemently. "We forget that it was, if not a revolution, at least a series of skirmishes. Take the Highway Sixty-one case, look what happened to Harry Prough. And he didn't defend the actual kidnappers, remember—his clients were charged with conspiracy.''

Prough had been sentenced to four years in jail on multiple counts of contempt of court. The conspiracy trial judge had been a real fascist, much worse than the judge who'd tried the kidnapping case.

''The conspirators were pretty outrageous, though.'' Their cohorts had kidnapped the baby of a corporate vice president, threatening to burn it in retaliation for the corporation's manufacture of napalm. One of Prough's clients had challenged the vice president at trial, shouting, ''Your chemicals curl the skin right off Vietnamese babies. Why should your baby be exempt?''

''No law against being outrageous. And look at it a bit more globally,'' Clement urged. ''The Left made some bad acts—segregation, Vietnam—expensive by making them divisive. In that context, there was room for everyone from theorists to terrorists.''

Clement Kerrey, apologist for baby-kidnappers.

My father smoothed his apron. ''It seems rather cold to be doing a cost-benefit analysis. And unfortunately, the terrorist part of the continuum dismantled some very worthy organizations. If the Weathermen hadn't smashed the SDS, we might still have an apparatus for social change. We might still—''

''Hooey,'' Mother interjected. ''The SDS was too incremental, too *liberal*.'' Definitely an epithet. ''Helping blacks—I mean African-Americans—petition for neighborhood stoplights— *Stoplights!* You don't change the system one stoplight at a time.''

If she started talking general strike, I'd scream. I heard myself say, ''You can't change the system, period. Probably not then, definitely not now.'' It just came out, the proverbial rude noise in church. "It's too entrenched. Too many people have bought in." I should know.

"I would have to disagree strongly." As if in keeping with the strength of his disagreement, Clement squeezed his leg harder. "Back to the Highway Sixty-one trial for a moment. All right, it makes perfect sense to arrest the actual kidnappers. They have as a witness the girl whose house was used in the kidnapping." He stared at some spot behind me as if reading a teleprompter. "Although I found it disturbing that they closed the courtroom during her testimony."

Edward cut in. "The testimony itself was reported, they just didn't allow her to be photographed." His skin was flushed and his brows were lowered. "I mean, fuck, look who she was testifying against. You can't blame her for going into the witness protection program."

"Of course not." Clement's tone was a little chilly. "I just meant that it gave the judge a great deal of unimpeded—and unobserved—latitude."

Hershey continued frowning. "Prough's speech."

During his sentencing, the judge's gavel hammering to shut him up, Harry Prough had delivered a passionate and now-famous indictment of the judiciary in general and that judge in particular.

The actual kidnappers had ended up with lighter sentences than Highway 61 "conspirators" who'd claimed to have no knowledge of the kidnapping plans.

My father shook his head. "Baby, you say we can't change the system—and maybe right now we can't. But don't you think it's a dialectic? We may be on the downswing at the moment—"

"You'd change things if you could, Willa." Clement sounded a little desperate. "You'd help if you knew what to do."

He couldn't be asking if I still felt pity for displaced Salvadorans and migrant farm workers? I scanned the row of pictures behind him—men loading boxes, families picking tomatoes, women canning shrimp. I thought of the old union organizing song, *Which side are you on, boys, which side are you on?*

"Karma yoga," Clement continued. "Maybe it doesn't make sense to hit the streets in this political climate—"

Mother piped her outrage. "Why do you say that?"

"—but we can still speak through our work."

I could feel four pairs of eyes on me.

When I'd taken the Wailes, Roth job, Mother had punched all my carefully programmed buttons, recited the radical catechism, watered me with a mother's tears. Still my knee had refused to jerk.

Maybe if I'd told them how much I hated the job—that it was like being slowly smothered in bankruptcy codes, that my coworkers had all the élan of well-dressed geckos—it would have partially restored their faith in me. I had made a point of telling them I merely represented banks and corporations in their byzantine dealings with other banks and corporations; that my ninety thousand a year was relatively untainted (even supposing my morals were worth that sum). It's not like big firms dirty their shoes by stepping on little people; there's not enough money in it.

I looked at my parents, thought about their years in the Peace Corps, their eleven convictions, their low-on-the-food-chain diet.

"We're canceled out," I insisted. "You guys don't see it because you hang around with other people just like you. But most of society eats Brazilian beef from cleared rain forests and doesn't bat an eye. Most of society doesn't care what kind of weapons or poisons it manufactures for a salary."

"So we shouldn't care, either?" Hershey was snide. Mr. Activism. A two-bit detective, a civil litigation whore.

"My point is, what's the use of just doing something? If it doesn't accomplish anything? If it doesn't make a dent?"

"How do you know that until you do it?" my father said quietly.

As if, after billing two thousand hours, I had energy to fritter away on long shots. "It's just so easy to believe you're effecting change when everyone around you agrees. Then you go out into the real world . . ."

I absentmindedly fingered a library book beside me on the couch. A biography of Mr. Compromise himself, Hubert Humphrey.

"Your father's reading it," Mother snorted. She tolerated his open-mindedness as another wife might tolerate philandering. "Such a chip-on-the-shoulder book. All those half-a-loaf liberals are ashamed of themselves for what they didn't do in the sixties and seventies."

"And radicals are ashamed of what they did do," I added.

My mother shot me a look.

I stifled a sudden urge to flee. I'm probably not the first woman to react that way to half an hour of her parents' company.

On the other hand, it was a luxury to talk politics. In L.A., people discuss their possessions, not their beliefs.

"So how was your trip?" My father's slide into small talk was forced, at best.

I gave them the guidebook rap on Big Sur and Seventeen Mile Drive. I didn't actually remember much except cars honking at my cowardly pace.

Throughout my monologue, Clement scowled and tapped his foot, possibly rehashing the prior conversation.

Mother's lips pursed into a sphincter of wrinkles. She's the kind of chalk-skinned blonde whose skin withers like dried fruit. I supposed mine would, too, by and by.

My father kept glancing at her, his pale blue eyes brimming with warning and worry. When he finally caught her eye, he raised his chin slightly. She raised hers, too. Damn: their take-us-away-we're-ready look.

No one spoke when I concluded. Finally, I asked my dad, "Have you seen Lissa?"

He sighed, a defeated droop to his bony shoulders. He'd followed my train of thought, I'm afraid. (He always had: condoms on my fourteenth birthday, briefcase on my thirtieth, hookah on my thirty-fifth.)

Lissa had been my teacher at the Haight Street Alternative School. I'd been shuttled to her place every time my parents were arrested. Eleven times I'd waved away clouds of incense and listened to her gush about how committed and noble my parents were. Other kids read *The Wind in the Willows*, I got *Civil Disobedience*; other kids watched *Bonanza*, I got *Harvest of Shame*. Legal conferences, defense funds, rallies—Patty Hearst never got so brainwashed.

"Lissa's still there," my father said. "She's had to shift her focus a little—infant dance and bilingual—but she's still there. Renamed the school."

"The Daniel Berrigan Home for Political Orphans?"

It wasn't much of a joke, but Mother's response was surprisingly negative. She stiffened, breath suddenly and audibly checked. She locked eyes with my father. If I hadn't known her so well, I'd have said she looked apprehensive. And that wasn't like her. Arrested eleven times, she'd never displayed apprehension; she'd always ridden bravely to the guillotine.

"Are you guys okay?" I hated to ask in front of Hershey; felt unprivate, invaded. Why the hell did he have to be here?

My father's forehead puckered, then smoothed back out. He stood. "Not if we don't eat soon. I don't know about the rest of you, but I'm starved."

Mother continued blinking at him, her face crumpling with indecision. Finally she stood, too.

Well, fine. Whatever they were into this time, let someone else press them to accept half a loaf of good sense. They could send me postcards from jail.

Sure.

I angled myself next to my father as we filed into the dining room. I kept my voice low. "Are you guys in trouble again?" The *again* came out a little shrill.

He didn't meet my eye. He just said, "No, no."

Then he looked at Clement Kerrey.

And Clement looked over my shoulder.

I followed the chain of glances to Edward Hershey, walking a few steps behind me. If communication had taken place between him and Clement, it was now over.

Edward grinned down at me. "It's great being back here. Your folks are so welcoming. They always make me feel like part of the family."

Part of the family. I could have smacked him.

4

M Y LANDLORD GREETED me with the brusque question, "So you're finally through with all that corporate nonsense?"

Ben Bubniak was a tall, unbent seventy-year-old with lank shoulder-length hair and watery blue bug-eyes. He was conservatively dressed in a Star Trek T-shirt and Navy surplus bell-bottoms. He was a lifelong friend of the family, and I used to spend hours in his apartment watching old movies on his VCR. Tonight, I just wanted to skip the amenities and pick up my keys. I just wanted to go upstairs and feel sorry for myself because I couldn't get stoned.

"Glad you're back, kiddo." Ben said so, but he didn't look glad. "Although Kali worked out great. Miss her already."

My former sublessee was a fellow red-diaper baby. She was a law student at Malhousie. She'd recently brought suit against the school, charging it with gender-based enroll-mentdiscrimination—probably the only sin that could not properly be laid at Malhousie's door.

I'd installed her in my apartment like a woman offering her dissatisfied mate a geisha. My parents and my landlord had been crazy about her.

I scanned Ben's apartment. I used to find it charming, with its walls of pulp science-fiction posters and its incongruous Victorian furniture. Right now, I was beyond finding anything charming. I'd tossed the sunny side of my conscious-ness off a pier.

"Did my new furniture arrive?"

Ben nodded, his hoary brows lowered, looking like an angry Moses.

"Good." I'd refurnished my apartment with a Macy's cat-alog and a long-distance phone call. As far as I was con-cerned, credit was the ultimate luxury. It wasn't what Thoreau had in mind, but more than anything else I'd ever experi-enced, it made life simple.

Ben rooted my keys out of a desk drawer jammed with pamphlets, polished crystals, and old diskettes. "Need help taking your things up?"

"No. I'll wait till morning to unpack my car."

"Yes, I heard you got yourself a car."

I slipped the ring of house keys off his crooked finger before he could ask if I'd "bought American."

I hadn't thought about factory closings in Flint, Michigan, until after I'd driven my Honda off the lot. Me, a former union labor lawyer. That was another reason I'd decided to flee Wailes, Roth: I risked becoming a Republican by osmosis.

5

I RAPPED ON the oak door before pushing it open. I felt nervous, walking into judge's chambers. As recently as two weeks ago, judge's chambers meant talking my way out of or into some transaction. It meant being completely on, completely here now. *Be Here Now*: ironic that I'd done Baba Ram Dass proud only in that context.

The Honorable Michael J. Shanna sat behind his plateau-sized desk, pale brows pinched together over a freckled potato of a nose and a wide Irish mouth.

"Judge?" I sounded deferential. More deferential than his other clerk, which bothered me. I seemed to be getting wimpier every year. "You asked me to remind you that you have a hearing in ten minutes."

The judge clasped his hands behind his head and stretched. "Thank you, Willa."

Behind him, shelves of legal reporters rose from floor to ceiling like a photographer's backdrop. I balanced a stack of file folders on a corner of the desk beside his shrine to Saint Jimmy the Uncharismatic. I wondered how he could stand to look at the hinged triple portrait of Carter every day. Carter with Judge Shanna and Clement Kerrey, among others, Carter with Sadat and Begin, Carter with 167 teeth showing.

"Judge? The Harry Prough hearing? Do you mind if I sit in?"

"Not at all. He's quite colorful—gets very overwrought. You'll enjoy it."

He reached for the opinion atop the files. He always had his mind made up before a hearing, my co-clerk had told me bitterly. No point waiting to draft the appropriate documents.

He reread the opinion, nodding. "This would wake them up over at the Ninth Circuit."

The judge had a reputation for having his Fourth Amendment rulings overturned. That was one of the reasons I'd jumped at the chance to clerk for him. He retained a nostalgic belief that the prohibition against unlawful search and seizure still meant something. It didn't matter how often the post-Reagan court reminded him that cops can break down your door and seize your possessions on a mere, sadistic whim. These days, the Fourth Amendment and a dollar will buy you a cup of coffee.

"There's something I'd like to discuss with you first." He pulled a white envelope out of his desk drawer. "The Hon. Michael J. Shanna," no address, was typed across the front.

As he slid a finger under the flap, there was a rap at the door.

The judge glanced at the envelope, then at me. He slipped it back into his desk, saying, "This afternoon will do."

My fellow clerk strode into the room. He'd been with the judge six months. The judge liked his clerks' tenure to overlap, rather than having two new ones every year.

George McLeod was the kind of bearded Yalie who believed in Rational Discourse and (if it could be achieved with understated good taste) martial law.

My first hour on the job, he'd made a point of telling me why he'd been hired. He'd been hired, he said, because he was the only conservative who'd applied.

Conservative Yalies generally applied to one of a zillion old coots on district and state court benches. Liberals had a harder time finding a niche. Most Democrat-appointed federal judges had been winnowed off the bench in the last ten years. Three state supreme court liberals had been recalled in a backlash referendum my parents called The Defenestration.

By way of further explanation, George had offered, "Did you ever notice Justice Douglas's opinions, how idiotic they became as years went by?"

William O. Douglas, Supreme Court Justice in the days when amendments were amendments. "He was so old."

George waved my observation aside. "He was unchallenged. Well, certainly he was challenged by other justices, but I mean in his writing. In his thinking, in chambers. You need at least one person around you who thinks you're wrong about everything. It keeps you articulating. It keeps you from thinking in shorthand. That's why Judge Shanna hired me. He's actually, for all his liberal biases, an extremely scrupulous jurist."

George took his devil's advocate function seriously and, as a result, was very tedious company.

Now, standing beside me in chambers, he again performed his (probably) self-chosen role. "Judge, if I may offer my interpretation of recent case law?"

I watched the judge listen gravely—not merely politely—to George's irrefutable catalog of supreme and appellate court cases castrating the Fourth Amendment.

Did George think the judge was an idiot? His opinion (which I'd spent my first two days of work drafting) went through the cases one by one, distinguishing them from the case before him. It was the "scrupulous jurist's" way of being radical.

But I suppose George had a compulsion to express his views, even against all odds and at the last possible moment. After a lifelong association with cranks, I understand that impulse. Cranks are certain their opinions are too urgent and too important to stifle. That's why we have a legal system, to ritualize the persuasion process and keep cranks from ripping each other's tongues out.

Judge Shanna stood. "Duly noted, George."

I glanced across the room at a wall of windows overlooking Civic Center traffic. I had a sudden urge to be outside, away from the intricacies of work relationships, away from the dust of law books and the smell of air-conditioned wool. My first week, and already I was sick of it.

Beside me, George sighed. I knew he was champing at the bit to begin work in a tax law firm. But then, he was less than a year out of law school. He didn't know lawyers routinely trade their private lives (including, in the case of male lawyers, their sex drives) for high-octane careers.

The judge disappeared into the "robing room"—basically a walk-in closet—connecting his chambers to the courtroom. He returned a moment later, smoothing the folds of his black robe over a wide torso that might have been muscle or might have been fat.

His court clerk stepped in, clearing his throat for the "All rise" with which he would enter the courtroom.

The judge picked up the case files, saying, "Ready, Freddy."

The two men disappeared into the robing room.

"You know he'll be overruled." George's thin, tidily bearded face was somber. "It's a waste of resources."

"The American Revolution was a waste of resources. The Boston Tea Party. That's what resources are for."

"Twist everything around to what you believe in the first place. Especially if it's expensive to do so. The liberal creed."

I'm a magnet for these guys. Maybe it's karmic, related to some past-life offense. Me and Bakunin blew up one bureaucrat too many.

I sighed. "George, I don't care if taxes are squandered on Stealth bombers or on endowments to the arts. I told you before, I'm completely"—or at least increasingly— "apolitical."

"Apolitical." He snorted derisively. "You wouldn't be here if you weren't a vouched-for Democrat."

A vouched-for Democrat. Talk about slander.

6

I SLID QUIETLY through the robing-room door into the courtroom, taking a seat in the empty jury box. The room, with its gray carpet, tall bench, huge flags and great seals, had an aura of cold justice. In a chilly courtroom one floor up, I'd once been sentenced to sixty days in jail. The judge who'd sentenced me was still on the federal bench. Judge Rondi had hated me in '71, when my lawyer unsuccessfully defended my suggestion that a Presidio M.P. go fuck himself. Rondi had hated me still more in '88, when my own lawyerly (and extra-lawyerly) maneuverings forced him to suspend the jail sentence of my activist client. Now I'd be running into him two or three times a week. Wouldn't that be pleasant?

The Hon. Michael J. Shanna, imposingly judicial in robe and black hornrims, was peering curiously at Harry Prough.

Prough had just stated his appearance, handing the court reporter his card so that she'd spell his name (pronounced *Pro*) correctly. Seated at the table behind him was a big man whose features might have been sensual if there'd been a flicker of animation behind them. He wore an ill-fitting and out-of-style suit, but he didn't squirm in it, didn't tug at it, didn't seem to care. He'd been pulled over in his car, supposedly for making a "rolling" stop.

He'd really been pulled over (according to Prough's moving papers) for being Tom Rugieri, former honcho in Highway 61. Whatever Clement Kerrey chose to think about its place in the lefty gestalt, Highway 61 for years did nothing but make bombastic threats against government property and personnel. It wasn't goaded into snatching the "fascist" baby of a corporate vice president until confronted with the flamboyant criminality of the Weathermen and the Symbionese Liberation Army. But Highway 61's kidnapping had gotten little press—it lacked the sex appeal of an heiress turned bank robber. The kidnapped baby was returned unharmed a day or two later. A handful of people were arrested. Rugieri—fresh meat for a right-wing judge—spent almost twenty years shunted from one federal prison to another, supposedly due to overcrowding, more likely just to harass him.

A few weeks after his release from the "correctional facility" in Pleasanton, California, police officers—six of them—searched Rugieri's car and found an M-16 rifle in the trunk. The gun was army-issue, government property, and the prosecution decided to make a federal case of it. The defendant claimed he kept the gun "to scare raccoons out of the garbage." Alluding to the Yippie weapon of choice, he'd added, "It's much more effective than cream pies."

Without the rifle as evidence, the prosecution's case vaporized. Harry Prough had moved to exclude the gun as the fruit of an illegal search. All week, law enforcement officials had gesticulated and orated for news cameras, channeling Adolf Hitler's anticrime speeches and evoking specters of marauding radicals and Banks of America in flames. "Certain liberal judges," a U.S. attorney had sneered, "would leave us once again vulnerable to the unrestrained hooliganism of the nineteen-sixties!" As if most of the hooligans hadn't worn badges and carried nightsticks.

"Your Honor," Harry Prough said now, "it has come to my attention that charges are being filed against my client in state court—"

"Your Honor"—the prosecutor hugged himself—"I was about to bring that up. In the interest of avoiding duplicative action—"

"I'd like to know what the—what's going on here. This is out-and-out persecution of my client!" Prough raised a skinny arm as if chastising the gods. "First the derogation of his rights and now this raft of contradictory charges in two separate courts—"

"Hardly contradictory!" The prosecutor looked like a sweaty tomato. "The weapon found in the defendant's trunk has been connected to certain illegal acts—"

"What? What illegal acts? Sniping, for godsake? How can the state pretend to connect this weapon to a drive-by crime in which no bullets or shells were recovered and no one saw a damn—"

"I am only concerned with the matter before *this* court, Mr. Prough." Shanna's voice boomed out like a kettledrum, even in the acoustically inferior room.

"Which brings me to what I've been trying to say, Your Honor." The prosecutor's brows sank gloomily. "In light of the charges against the defendant in state court, we now move to dismiss the federal action against him."

Dismiss. I heard a hubbub in the pews. The legal reporter from the *Examiner* had risen, to the apparent consternation of tired-looking yuppies behind her. Two men in tight suits and striped ties were pushing their way out the massive courtroom doors. Not lawyers—lawyers shop at better stores. Plainclothes cops, I assumed.

Harry Prough shook his head as if to clear it. I didn't blame him for being befuddled. What was the government trying to prove? Why dismiss this case? Why not hit Rugieri from both sides, state and federal?

Prough's voice was tight. "Your Honor, it's obvious the prosecution believes an adverse ruling on the motion before this court will affect the outcome of the state court action." He pointed at the prosecutor, defying him to disagree. "If this court rules the search was illegal, it will be much harder to convince a state court otherwise—much harder for the state to get the rifle admitted into evidence. This is a cynical attempt by the prosecution to cut its losses here and find a friendlier venue—one it can sway with anti-sixties rhetoric and right-wing bogeymen. It's the worst kind of forum-shopping, Your Honor. It's outright abuse of process!"

Right on.

"Mr. Prough!" Shanna raised a small, pale hand.

In the long, quiet moment that followed, I stared at Prough. His thin lips were compressed, his eyes narrowed. If he was mistrustful of government, he certainly had cause. The last time he defended Rugieri, he ended up in jail for contempt of court.

When I saw him four years later at a rally in San Francisco (maybe the last I ever attended), his curly black hair had turned gray and deep worry lines were etched into his face. He joined Charles Garry's law firm, but was asked to leave because (rumor had it) he verbally abused associates.

"Mr. Prough," Shanna repeated. "If the prosecution wishes to dismiss its action against your client, I don't see how you can have the audacity to complain. Surely you prefer to defend him once, rather than twice.''

Someone in the pews moaned. I glanced back. And felt like I'd been kicked in the stomach.

The plainclothes cops had reentered the room, and there was a third man with them. He was standing behind the last pew staring at me. His low-browed, swarthy face was expressionless except for a shocked slackness of jaw and (was I imagining it?) a hooded sadness of the eyes.

Don Surgelato.

I quickly looked away, staring blindly at the judge.

The judge was saying to the prosecutor, ''Your motion to dismiss this action is hereby granted. Please submit the appropriate order to my clerk by tomorrow morning.''

Don Surgelato. I could feel the rocketing jolt—explosive, chemical, visceral.

Scientists have done experiments with laboratory rats showing they will press drug- rather than food-dispensing levers over and over again until they die. Romance is like that for me—I hit the wrong lever every time. Every time. Damn.

7

I STOOD IN the cool, gray-carpeted corridor. I watched other judges' clerks click along in their black pumps, chins held high, file folders clutched to their lapels. They looked so polished, so straight; made me feel like a hippie in bad drag.

I'd slipped out of my juror's chair. I'd gone into the robing room, through the judge's chambers, through the reception area, past the office I shared with George, into the corridor, and through the door leading to the public corridor. I must have done all that; I was out here now. I was standing near a desk manned by a security guard, looking at the public entrance to Judge Shanna's courtroom. I was watching people leave, some stifling yawns, some laughing and chatting, some with the cranky, preoccupied look of busy lawyers.

I wondered why Don Surgelato had shown up at this hearing. Did he know I worked for Shanna now? Had he come to see me? (He'd had a year to call me, and he hadn't made the effort.)

But he'd spotted me in the courtroom. It would seem unsociable not to say hello. Like I'd been carrying a torch, and gotten burned by it.

I tried to ease the cramp out of my shoulders. No big deal; I'd extend my hand to him and say something appropriate. I'd spent the last year of my life saying appropriate things to men just as august as the lieutenant of homicide, hadn't I?

In fact, I'd spent the last decade being appropriate—convincing Stanford University and Malhousie Law School to credential me, convincing two law firms and a real-life judge to hire me. As long as I looked the part and watched my mouth, I was okay. I might not have poise, but I had a wardrobe.

Besides, I'd invested serious money in understanding my reaction to Don Surgelato. I'd spent maybe ten therapy hours talking about the nonromance. (At eighty-five dollars an hour, maybe I should have bought an inflatable doll and squandered the difference.) I'd learned that my reaction to Don Surgelato was "powerful" (in therapist-speak) because he had done the one thing my parents had always refused to do: he'd violated his moral code to protect me. Instead of behaving as the lieutenant of San Francisco's homicide detail should, he'd killed someone just to keep me safe, just to keep a family secret of mine.

Unfortunately, the (rather expensive) insight didn't change my reaction.

I stood rooted when the courtroom door opened and Don pushed through.

He closed the distance between us, offering his hand in the calm way I'd meant to offer mine.

"Willa," he said, like a stoic man confronting an old problem. Like a man saying "bursitis" or "more rain."

I shook his hand. We both let go sooner than was strictly polite. I saw a flash of colored stone as he threaded his left hand into his pocket. A class ring?

A beat or two after I should have spoken, he said, "Are you working for Judge Shanna?"

I remember when I didn't consider Don handsome. When I first met him, after the murder of a law school classmate, I saw a tough-looking cop of obvious Italian extraction. On the short side, broad-chested, short-legged, low brows, close-set eyes, nose flattened by an old break.

"Yes. My first week."

He nodded. "You look good. L.A. agreed with you?" Brown eyes, dimpled chin, curly hair, full lips. It was just a matter of focus.

"It agreed with my résumé."

Why was the ring on his left hand?

Don glanced over his shoulder as a tiny woman in an obvious blond wig pushed through the courtroom door. She hurried by me, head shaking slightly. She flattened herself against the wall beside the elevator, as motionless as a bas relief.

I was reminded of something a partner at Wailes, Roth once told me: predators go after animals that call attention to themselves. Speaking of a hard-ass judge, he'd warned, "Flutter and flail, and he'll think of you as dinner." With her blond wig and beige clothes, this woman was stock still, blending in.

Don lowered his voice. "You heard the investigation came out okay?"

I nodded. The favor Don had done me—killing a murderer who'd possessed information that would have fried my mother—the favor had cost him. There had been a homicide investigation of the shooting; there had been police, citizens advisory board, and civil service commission proceedings; there had been anti-Surgelato rallies organized by my mother, among others. He'd taken a lot of abuse, he'd weathered a career maelstrom. For me. And how many lab rats could say that?

"You're okay?" he asked.

"Yes."

"Well," he said more loudly. He acted as if it were time to go. But he didn't go. "You want to get some coffee or something?"

"Yes. Oh, no. I can't now. After work?"

He nodded. Then shook his head. "I'm tied up till late."

Tied up. The closest I'd come to a date lately was a paramedic who kept hinting he could get "soft restraints."

"Late's okay." I was noticing anatomical contours that other federal clerks, in their vast dignity, would not.

He continued to hesitate. Making arrangements would make it seem less casual, more significant. Not like meeting an acquaintance in a corridor and having a quick cup of coffee.

Part of me wanted to say, Well, okay, let's skip it. Part of me wanted to say what he wanted to hear. That's the essence of poise, after all.

The other part of me wanted to see him again. Get him into soft restraints, if possible.

"You could come by my place after work." Flail and flutter—I knew immediately that it was the wrong thing to say. He leaned backward, away from me. "Or how about that restaurant at Haight and Masonic? They have good espresso."

He looked disturbed, almost guilty. "Around nine thirty? Is that too late for you?"

"That's fine."

He nodded. Stood there, executing an uncomfortable shuffle of the feet. He leaned toward me. For a minute I thought he was going to give me a social embrace.

The courtroom was still emptying, people emerging alone or in murmuring pairs.

Don straightened, extending his right hand again. (Left still in his pocket.) As I took his hand, he glanced at the beige woman, still flattened against the wall. His grip became suddenly tight.

Behind him, Harry Prough ushered Tom Rugieri out of the courtroom. They were head to head, frowning, not looking around, Rugieri listening to whispered counsel with full intensity. For a second he reminded me of Don, broad, dark-haired, skin the pale tan of a sun-starved Mediterranean. But Rugieri's facial expression was different, clenched with bitterness. His shoulders climbed to his neck as Prough gesticulated with the hand that didn't hold the briefcase.

As they approached the elevator, the beige woman sidled away, turning with quick steps down the corridor. Rugieri glanced at her back, stopping short. Prough went through the open door, and a moment later Rugieri followed.

Don dropped my hand.

8

I SAT IN my office, staring at George McLeod's empty chair.
George was off researching something about junk bonds.
He'd left with the bitter comment that it didn't matter anyway, the judge would just ignore his (save-the-resources)
conclusion.

I looked at the three walls of books, the big windows
overlooking the Civic Center, the back-to-back desks strewn
with briefs and memos and rows of file folders trapped between metal bookends. The judge had a huge caseload, but
that only meant extra work—not the tension and pressure of
being a low-level associate. There was an air of calm about
the office, of time for adequate research and reasoned advice.
Not that pinched nerve of worry: of partners bursting in to
complain and to bully, of frantic phone calls and court ap-
pearances off the cuff.

I sat in my comfortable chair, federal reporters open in front of me, feeling like a student again.

Six or seven months' reprieve. Then I'd have to figure out what I really wanted to do, launch another volley of résumés. Maybe by then the prospect of practicing law would not give me the dry heaves.

I was startled by the buzz of my telephone. Even more startled to hear Edward Hershey's voice on the line.

"W.J., listen, I really need your help. That favor I told you about? Couldn't you be a pal, just this one time? It's really important." His voice wheedled, flirted; pure Hershey.

"If you do me a favor first."

"Oh, God, anything." I was surprised by the raw relief in his voice.

"But you have to do it right now. I'm not sure how—I guess public records. You've only got a couple of hours until government offices close, but it has to be this afternoon."

"Okay, really. Anything. Command me."

"I need to know if somebody's married."

Hesitation. Then, "Can I ask why?"

"No."

"Okay. Doesn't matter. But does it have to be today? If it's not a Santa Cruz marriage, or lack thereof—"

"San Francisco. It has to be today. Before nine thirty tonight."

"San Fran—sure. I can phone a friend to do my legwork. You got a name for me?"

Maybe I shouldn't. Maybe this wasn't the right way to find out. More to the point, maybe this wasn't the man to find out for me. Edward was smart. No chance he wouldn't know what it meant.

"Tell me your favor first."

"Look, Willa, it won't take you more than an hour or two, I swear it. It's just talking to somebody for me."

"Talking about what?"

"It's not that big a deal, honest. So give me the name. Who's the married guy?"

I had qualms about Edward's favor. My favor, too. But nothing like the qualms I should have had.

"Willa? You got a name for me, babe?"

"Don't call me babe."

"If you're worried about my favor, really, it's not that big a deal. Nothing you can't—"

"All right." I'd worry about his damn favor later, when I had some worry to spare. "It's Don Surgelato."

"As in Lieutenant, SFPD Homicide Detail?"

"Yes." I listened to him breathe. "Can you find out before tonight?"

"Yeah, Willa, sure."

"I'll talk to you later about your favor, okay?"

"You, um, got pretty close to Surgelato, huh? When he caught Warneke's killer."

"No."

"I followed the brouhaha about the shooting. Your mom organized some of the rallies against him, didn't she?"

In her spare time, when she wasn't making the world safe for vegetarian neosocialism.

"And I should just find out if he's married? Anything else?"

"Or if his divorce— I'm not sure if he was divorced or legally separated or what." I'd met his (former?) wife once. A busty brunette with an intelligent face, a brittle laugh, sad eyes. Maybe that came from loving a man who didn't know if he wanted you. Maybe I had a brittle laugh and sad eyes, too.

"Whatever records they have."

"Whatever records."

"Willa?"

"Yes?"

"When can you come down here and do this thing for me?"

"I don't know."

"Saturday? Or could you make it sooner?"

"Saturday."

"Okay. Call you before five with the scoop on the Surge."

"Edward, if you tell anyone about this—"

"Discretion is my middle name," he assured me.

I would have suggested something more apt, but I didn't want to use profanity in my place of employment.

9

AN HOUR LATER, I was standing in Judge Shanna's chambers saying, "Shit."

The judge coughed mildly, leaning back in his leather chair. "Naturally, I don't give credence to this kind of thing." He didn't sound like it was a bit natural. In fact, it sounded more like a question than a statement.

I held a sheet of white bond paper. I hadn't checked its watermark, but I knew it was Democracy Bond. The typeface looked boringly standard, but I knew it was Imperial, the "proud innovation" of an electronic-memory typewriter corporation.

I knew because I'd seen this typeface on this kind of paper before. I'd seen it two years ago in a stack of anonymous hate mail addressed to me at my apartment: the letters Edward Hershey had traced for me.

I looked at Judge Shanna. Would he believe me if I told him who'd sent those letters?

I stared down at the unsigned sheet in my hand. I read it again:

It has come to my attention that you have selected as your clerk a young woman who was arrested for murder in February of last year and who in addition served a full sixty-day sentence (no time reduction for good behavior) in 1971.

Let me direct your attention to your own article in the *Malhousie Law Review*, Spring 1985: "I have been called overscrupulous in matters regarding points of judicial propriety. In fact, it has been hinted that I am 'overscrupulous' in matters of form to mask a 'radicalism' of judicial philosophy. . . . I can only respond with a jurist's outrage at the suggestion that 'form' is somehow a mere handmaiden of the judicial process. Indeed, strict propriety, as well as *avoidance of the appearance of impropriety* are the very infrastructure of our system of jurisprudence." [Italics mine.]

I marvel therefore at your choice of a former convict and two-time arrestee who has demonstrated a distinct lack of respect for the values you are sworn to defend. As a matter of moral principle and judicial decorum, you should reconsider your selection of this woman Willa Jansson. Her clerkship is a stain upon the court system.

In the town that gave us Dan White, I was a stain on the fucking court system.

"I am outraged, of course, that something like this should be anonymous," the judge said somberly.

Was it the "something like this" or the anonymity that

bothered him, I wondered. "You knew about the two arrests, Judge?"

"Actually, no, I did not."

They were part of my record for anyone who cared to delve into the matter. But he didn't expect me to put something like that on my résumé?

"I was arrested in an antiwar protest at the Presidio in nineteen seventy-one." I shrugged. "Judge Rondi sentenced me to two months. Seventy-three other people were arrested, but I'm the only one who appeared before Rondi. I'm the only one who got jail time." I tried not to sound bitter toward his fellow federal judge. But I'd spent two months in airless rooms, being shouted at and prodded and herded and strip-searched and forced for God knows what reason to sew blue curtains, endless blue curtains in a room full of sobbing women. "As for the recent arrest, it was a mistake. Charges were dropped and I was released within twenty-four hours." After Don Surgelato shot and killed Julian Warneke's real killer.

The judge waved a freckled hand, as if to say the details didn't matter. But I noticed he'd waited until I finished. "I am more disturbed, as I said, by the fact of this letter. By its animus."

He watched me hawkishly.

I watched him back. I couldn't do it. He'd never believe me, not on so slight an acquaintance. He'd never believe the letter came from the typewriter of the Honorable Manolo M. Rondi, U.S. District Court. He'd never believe the letter was from the Honorable anybody. He had too much invested in believing in the integrity of federal judges.

I said, "I was involved in the investigation of a—of some murders." No use providing a list. "I got quite a bit of anonymous hate mail then, unfortunately. I, um"—how to ring the right bell?—"I came to realize that I have no control over the animus of strangers, of people who are more interested in sensationalism than the truth.''

"Quite right. And I'm not laying this at your door." He scowled, face turned so that he regarded me sidelong. "I merely thought you should be aware of it."

He held out his hand for the letter.

It was all I could do not to hold it up, not to check for the Democracy watermark. Not to explain about the Imperial typeface. About the warranty registration card Manolo Rondi had sent the typewriter company.

I watched the judge ostentatiously crumple the letter and drop it into a wastebasket emblazoned with the U.S. seal.

I waffled a moment longer. God damn that miserable Rondi, anyway. But I'd already used the hate letters against him once. I'd threatened to make them public. And he'd been uncharacteristically (and uncoincidentally) lenient in sentencing my client, a vociferous activist who'd failed to register with the selective service.

I'd blackmailed a federal court judge, in fact—something I did not think Shanna would applaud. It definitely behooved me to keep my mouth shut.

So much for my tension-free workplace.

I dashed out of chambers. I dashed past Margaret the receptionist and slammed myself into the office I shared with George.

George was back. "Is the judge free?"

"Drastically reduced."

George rose, rotating his shoulders as if to ease a crick. "You got a call. I took a message." He pointed to a square of pink paper on my desk.

I glanced down. The call was from Edward Hershey.

10

So it wasn't a surprise when Don Surgelato stopped stirring his *lattè* and said, "I don't know if I mentioned I got remarried. To Tina. You met her, didn't you? At my place once?"

"Yes." The wall behind him was decorated with china plates, dozens of them. I feigned a sudden fascination with them.

Yes, I'd met Tina. She'd complained that "Donnie" hated to see her have fun at parties, that he expected her to slave in the kitchen like a good Italian wife; that he'd left her to punish her. She'd had a stack of college textbooks with her. Don had carried them down to her car. Just like in high school, she'd said.

How could I compete with a bond dating back to high school? The longest I'd kept a relationship together was ten months, the last third of it in pitched battle over Reaganomics.

To me, decades-long attachments seemed excessive, almost neurotic. I wondered if I could persuade him of that.

"Six months ago." He put his coffee spoon down on the white tablecloth. The class ring glinted dull silver with a smooth blue stone. "We did it six months ago."

"How long had you been married? Before?"

"Nineteen years." He said it without pride or sentiment. If anything, he sounded embarrassed. "A hell of a thing, nineteen years. Hard to walk away from. You don't put your life back together in a way that makes sense, not really. Things seem mixed up and this person that you loved once, she gets . . ." He sighed. "You feel guilty. You feel lonely. You feel like it's kismet, you know; the two of you being together."

Kismet again. Maybe it was my kismet to feel like fresh road kill.

"How long were you separated?"

"Two years."

I sipped my coffee, scalding my tongue. We were surrounded by somber young people in berets, anemic-looking punks in black leather, a few middle-aged gays in nice jackets. The waitress wore extravagant stage makeup. Everyone but us was eating some kind of dessert.

He'd been married when I met him; his marriage breaking up, I supposed. It explained the tentative flirting on his part; needing to know a stranger could find him attractive.

He'd been single the next time we met. The flirting had stopped. But he'd grown to care about me. He must have, to have done what he did for me.

It must have been starting by then, the guilt and loneliness he described. He'd cared about me, yes; he'd kissed me, yes. But she'd been the one. Tina.

I had a sudden urge to go to a cowboy bar, drink to excess, pick a fight. It's never me, damn it. I'm never the important one.

"How about you, Willa?"

"Worked too hard last year. No dates, just cases."

"I know how that goes." A pained glance. (Small, deep-set eyes—funny they could be so expressive.) "I thought a lot about you."

"Did you?"

"Yes. Of course." He shook his head as if to emphasize an understatement. Or maybe I was wishing.

"I wondered if you had."

His jaw went slack, his brows twitched as if I'd hurt him. "I love my wife," he said. "But I think about you."

"Do you want—I mean, are you committed—"

"I'm committed to my wife." He stared at his coffee. "It's easy to screw up a marriage. I've done it. And paid for it. I'm not going to do it again. Tina couldn't take it."

I ended up lying. "I respect that."

It was what a federal clerk should say. And I owed him a favor, I knew that.

"Are you okay?"

"Don't worry about me." Motto of the unimportant.

"I'll call you. We'll do this every once in a while."

"Sure." It's been swell.

11

EDWARD WAS WAITING for me when I got to work the next morning. He was leaning on the corridor wall next to the intercom, looking sleepy-eyed but tidy in gray slacks and a navy sport coat. He straightened when he saw me.

"Hello there, W.J."

I was carrying a cup of coffee from the sixteenth-floor cafeteria. I felt like hell. I'd been drinking white wine most of the night. I wasn't sure which type of morning-after was worse, the low-grade lingering pot high or the queasy ache of a hangover. But there are times when you need an anesthetic, whatever your next-day obligations. I'd have clubbed myself, if that was all I'd had on hand. I doubt my head would have felt any worse.

"It must be an important favor," I observed. A two-hour drive up from Santa Cruz, and it was barely eight A.M.

"Yeah. Talk in your office?"

I pressed the intercom button, noticing a faint twist of citrus in the air. I tried to remember if Edward had favored cologne back when. Instead I remembered, with disconcerting clarity, the musculature of his chest. Hormones, God—I was too old for this.

A voice filled the speaker. The judge's secretary.

"Morning, Margaret. It's Willa."

A buzzer sounded and I pushed open the massive door, guarding my coffee as Edward threaded by me.

We turned right, ignoring the warren of offices to the left: a workroom for the judge's student externs (when he had them), a Xerox room, separate entrances to the courtroom, the robing room, the judge's chambers. In either direction, corridors led to the multioffice quarters of other judges on this floor. Edward, with no overt rubbernecking, seemed intent on memorizing what he saw. Professional habit, perhaps.

I led him through the reception area, introducing him by name but not occupation to Margaret. "Is the judge in yet?"

"No. Nor George."

"If the judge needs me, interrupt." If the *janitor* needs me, interrupt.

I motioned Edward into the office I shared with George, closing the door behind us. Such a dignified place, with its smell of law books and its drab view of government buildings, a few still sporting post-quake plywood.

I sat at my desk and Edward pulled George's chair alongside it. For a minute he didn't speak, he just grinned at me. Grinned like we shared some secret.

I forget sometimes that we lived together. Those memories, potentially precious, had been ruined for me by what came after. But just for this moment, seeing Edward with a fond smile and the diffuse light of a city morning on his face, just for this rather hormonal moment, I let myself remember how it felt to be in love with him.

"So, kismet. Favors." I didn't want the moment to last.

"Kismet, right." The grin vanished. Edward has a square-jawed, crannied face—small eyes, bushy brows, pushed-around nose, thin lips. Nothing special if it weren't on a tall, long-legged, broad-shouldered man with lots of sexy curls and a trademark squint. "And favors. I guess you don't want to tell me what yours was about? With Surgelato."

The funny thing was, I did want to tell him. I missed my therapist; I missed talking about things that mattered to me. But therapists are paid to listen and not judge. Edward might offer his honest opinion, and I'm not into the painful truth. Not at eight in the morning.

"Idle curiosity," I lied. I flicked the plastic cap off my Styrofoam cup of coffee. I didn't know how many brain cells I'd pickled the night before—a bottle of Sauvignon Blanc's worth. Maybe the coffee would revive a few of them.

"Can I have a swallow of that?" Edward looked as tired as I felt.

"I guess."

I watched him sip the hot liquid. Wished I'd thought to check his lips for sores. (My therapist says I have a problem with trust.)

He handed back the cup, saying, "Well, it's like this."

I drank coffee and hoped it wouldn't be anything I hated doing. Had I but known, as the saying goes.

He sighed, crinkled his brows, rubbed his knuckles over his chin. "This friend of mine, rich litigator husband, big house— Her name's Rita, for Margarita, Delacort. Her husband's Phil Delacort." He paused as if expecting me to recognize the name. "Big wheel in Santa Cruz. Old money, you know, great-looking suits, hair like a Macy's catalog.'' He added, unnecessarily, ''I don't like him much.'' He scowled at the desktop, tapping it pensively. ''A very intellectual type guy. Uncaring, you might say. Obsessive.''

''Ergo a good lawyer.''

''Yeah. Great lawyer. Look, I'll be honest with you.'' He spread his hands as if to convince me of his candor. ''Rita and I were pretty close for a while. A long time ago. Then I did some work for Delacort, ran into her again by accident. Very surprised to see her, in fact.'' His tone and expression became noncommittal, unmoved. ''Also surprised by her situation—the house, the Stepford husband, wrapped up in her kids' gymnastics lessons. I mean, I knew her many, many moons ago.''

''So now she's a yuppie mom?'' I shrugged. ''What did you expect? We all changed.''

''Yeah.'' He stared out the window. ''She's been married like seven, eight years, two young kids, things okay on the surface. When Delacort's around. Kind of guy can be really charming and focused, except that he's usually focused on work. Which left her . . .''

''Lonely.''

''Feeling like she didn't matter.''

''Okay. I get it.''

''Look, Willa''—still staring out the window— ''I really cared about her. The affair we had, it messed her up, really confused her and left her, well . . . battered. And that wore me down—I was just a kid, really. I guess I was looking for an out, for something and somebody less draining. Somebody more fun.'' He smiled sadly, almost lovingly, at me.

''I don't need your life story, Edward. Could we fast-forward, please?''

''All of a sudden she's fed up with Delacort. Grabs her kids and goes tearing out of there. Won't go back.'' He met my eye. "I told her she could stay at my place for a while. Which is not a very good place for her."

Noble bastard. "I should be getting to work."

"She's panicking—about money, about what Phil will do. It's gotten to the point where it's eating her up." He ran his fingers through his curls.

I waited for him to cut to the chase. When he didn't, I crumpled my empty Styrofoam cup and dropped it into the wastebasket like a handful of coarse snow. I'd been listening to Edward for ten minutes and still didn't know what he wanted from me.

He stared out my wall of windows. "She needs somebody to go talk to Phil and find out what's on his mind."

"She can't call him?"

A wry smile. "She won't."

"And she doesn't have any friends that could do it for her?"

"Not really." A quick glance. "I can't because Delacort's a little . . . suspicious of me."

"Because his wife left him to move in with you? Touchy guy."

"And she doesn't want to bring in a full-fledged lawyer right now."

"Oh, thanks!"

"No, no, I didn't mean it like that. I mean, you know, not a divorce lawyer, not somebody who'd make Phil feel threatened. Nothing heavy at this point. She just wants someone to talk to him. An intermediary who speaks Phil's language. A lawyer, so Phil doesn't stomp all over her rights—demand the kids, shit like that—but—"

"Not a 'threatening' lawyer?"

"Right." He looked pleased that I'd caught on. "And it can't be anybody local. Nobody from Santa Cruz."

"Because Phil's a local big shot. I'm not completely slow."

His face turned pink; he looked distinctly uncomfortable. "So, okay? You'll talk to Rita? Figure out what to say to Phil?"

I stood. "Edward, I can't believe this. You came to me because you specifically did not want a full-fledged, threatening lawyer. And you haven't even told me what I'm supposed to do in my role as wimpy, second-rate mouthpiece."

He stood, too, bumping his knee on the side of my desk. "I wouldn't put it like that."

"It's kind of insulting—"

George McLeod chose that moment to throw open the door. He looked angry. "I'm sorry to interrupt, but I've been waiting fifteen minutes."

I looked at him, shaking my head. Waiting? Why had he been waiting? Why hadn't he walked in sooner?

Edward looked him up and down, then said to me, "Anyway, you already said you'd do it."

"For two hours," I amended. "Your favor couldn't have taken any longer than that. Okay? I'll give this thing two hours."

Edward scowled. Behind him, George flattened himself against the bookcase and sidled over to his desk, snatching back the chair Edward had displaced.

"Okay," Edward said finally. "An hour with her and an hour with him. Anything extra and I'll owe you."

"You already owe me."

George was looking extremely titillated, arms folded across his chest and brows up.

Edward turned so all George could see was his back. "You know what? That thing you've been so mad at me about? You keep forgetting it's my problem, too. In fact, I'd be willing to bet it's been a worse problem for me than for you."

Oh, great. Let's compare blisters in front of my coworker.

"Two hours," I repeated. "Call me at home and we'll set up a time."

He stood there a minute. "You promised you'd do it Saturday."

"So I'll see you Saturday. For two hours maximum."

"Okay. I'll call you."

The funny thing was, when he left I was sorry. I was getting pretty hard up for friends, I guess.

12

IN MOST SAN Francisco neighborhoods there's no trace of the earthquake. From the Golden Gate Bridge you see squashed blocks of the Marina district (including a house Julian Warneke had bequeathed my mother). South of Market you occasionally see a rubbly hole, as if a rowhouse had been teleported into space. A few Civic Center buildings are still eye-patched with plywood. And because they closed the Embarcadero Freeway, traffic resembles the tenth circle of hell.

But Santa Cruz is much worse. I was shocked to find the downtown street I remembered as a hip little arboretum looking like Dresden: gutted basements where buildings used to be, Cyclone fences and bulldozers blocking pedestrian access, the few remaining buildings pocked with fallen plaster. One street over, khaki vinyl pavilions covered parking lots, their signs announcing relocated businesses within. I didn't see anybody going into or out of them.

The rest of town looked pretty much as I recalled from forays in my teen years. Kids on bicycles balanced surfboards, retrohippies played music on sagging porches, purple-haired students sprawled on dry lawns. I had the impression, driving around, that most people were off at the beach; that no one could be bothered to weed or mend, not with the sun out and the waves high.

Edward Hershey's house shared that student-tenant look. It was in a neighborhood of miniature Queen Annes with rotting gingerbread. From a bagelry down the block came the perfume of morning coffee and crusty bread. I wanted to hang out. I wanted to smoke a joint at the beach. I wanted to renege on my promise.

In fact, I wish I had. I wish I hadn't stepped into a tidy living room and a hell of a mess.

A small-boned, dark-haired woman—presumably Rita Delacort—was crouched over a German shepherd as if over a dying lover. Tears glazed the freckles of her contorted face as Edward tried to pull her to her feet. She was saying, "Hasn't begged for food, hasn't bothered me, hasn't jumped at me with his constant dog demands. Why didn't I notice, why didn't I notice?"

"Rita, let go, come on," Edward urged. "We'll take him to the vet. It's probably nothing."

But when I saw the dog, eyes rolled back and mouth flecked with foamy spittle, I thought Edward was being optimistic.

Rita Delacort continued pulling at the dog's neck. "Friend! Come on, get up. Get up, boy. Oh, God, Friend, what did I let them do? It should have been a two-way street. I should have looked out for you, too." Then to Edward, "It must have been in some food. He'll eat anything, it's such a bummer that he'll eat—"

She rocked back on her heels and began to sob, one hand over her eyes and the other on the dog's chest.

I'd walked through the open door without knocking, so Edward glanced at me in considerable surprise. He didn't comment. He tossed me a set of keys and bent over the dog, saying, "Open up the back for me, Willa."

I caught the jingling mass, deducing they were car keys. I hesitated, wondering if I should or could offer greater support than unlocking car doors. The dog wriggled frantically, struggling for air. The room smelled of him, an unpleasant, swampy smell.

As I turned to leave, I heard Rita wail, "If he dies, it's my fault."

"Bullshit" was Edward's reply. I heard him grunt, as if hoisting the big dog. "Go pick up your kids. Don't worry."

"You don't understand. I went to see Tom. His court hearing."

Edward's voice was sharp, inches behind me. "Willa, Jesus! Move it."

I hurried out to unlock the back of a dirty, old-model Jeep.

Edward was right behind me, panting as he situated the dog over a small mountain of litter and oily towels.

As he walked around to the driver's side, I blocked his path.

"Do you still need the favor?" I felt decidedly *de trop*.

Edward glanced at the back of the Jeep, eyes brimming with anxiety. "Yes! God, yes. The trouble is—"

From the porch Rita called, "Oh please, Edward, go. *Go!*"

"It might be a problem getting her to communicate right now." He pushed me unceremoniously aside, throwing open the door. "Make her talk to you. Get Delacort's address, get up to his place. Soon as you can. This afternoon."

"What am I supposed to do there?"

He quickly slid in, slammed the door, engaged the engine. "Say anything. Just go." He ground the gears. "Promise."

"But I don't even know what I'm supposed to—"

Rita flew down the driveway and began pounding on the Jeep's hood. She looked like one of the Furies with her wild mantle of black curls. Even shorts and a halter top didn't spoil the effect. "Go! Hurry!"

"Just see what Delacort has in mind. And stop back here when you're done. I'll be back by then." He cast a worried glance at Rita. "Take care of her."

13

Inside Hershey's house, Rita Delacort paced. Paced and cried.

"Kids. I should pick them up. Oh, God. Should have gone with Edward."

"I gather that was your dog." Nothing like a penetrating observation.

"My second one." She stopped pacing, turned to me with burning cheeks and bright eyes. "Alonso was my first. A Vietnam vet, big shepherd, they cut his vocal cords so he could walk, point, and sniff out snipers without barking and giving away their position. He got old and the war ended, so they retrained him for civilians. Once when I lived in San Luis Obispo, Alonso chased someone out of my apartment, someone who'd been waiting inside." She ran a shaky hand through her curls. "I left town after that. I met Phil."

"That's your husband."

She laughed, the weakest, most humorless laugh I've ever heard. "Second dog, second husband. I got Friend nine years ago. Right before I met Phil. He's a good dog, a sweet dog, not as well trained as Alonso, but at least he doesn't try to attack Asians." Another laugh of sorts. "How am I going to feel safe without him?"

This was either a very dog-dependent or a (justifiably?) paranoid woman.

The latter possibility struck a chord in me. "People act like it's crazy to feel threatened." I shivered, remembering myself on the window ledge of Julian Warneke's office building, hiding from a killer. From a friend of mine. "But there's damn good cause sometimes."

"Yes." The word was an explosion of gratitude. She sank into a worn Herculon couch, hugging herself. "A long time ago I stayed with Edward. His apartment in Boston."

Boston. I stiffened. "When was that?"

"I'd been living by myself, but I got this phone call one day from my mother-in-law." Her shoulders hunched. "From my first marriage. The most beautiful woman, in her way— But mad at me, blaming me for things, calling me things." A long sigh. "I don't know how she tracked me down—I wasn't listed. Anyway, the point is, I thought I'd feel safer at a friend's, and I went to Edward's."

There was a long silence. I watched her face harden into something bland and distant.

"What year was this?" In 1971, when I left Boston for San Francisco (via the San Bruno jail), Edward had a love affair. He must have, to have acquired his sudden virus. Not that I should care now, care with whom. Water under the bridge.

"Year?" She shook her head. "I'd only been there a few

days when a man broke in.'' She swallowed several times.
''I had an uncle out here. In San Francisco. He sent me plane
fare, bought me Alonso.''

I sat opposite her on a crackled leather chair. ''It takes
something like that before people will believe you're not just
paranoid.''

She stared at her fingers, flexing and stretching them.
''That's the thing about Phil, you know, my husband. I feel
safe with him. I go back and forth about it. I'm not happy. I
don't love him. But I think about how it was all those years
before I met him. Scared all the time, feeling so out in the
open. Reclusiveness is the ultimate luxury, really. Privacy.''

I remembered throngs of reporters with their jostling questions, policemen in my face. Privacy. Hallelujah.

''My mother-in-law from my first marriage . . .'' Another
long silence. ''It feels wrong that I'm not married to him
anymore. Even after all this time. It feels wrong to say 'my
husband' and mean Phil. And Phil's mother—she'll never be
my mother-in-law, not like . . . Anyway my first mother-in-
law, she used to say, *'E peccati si piangone, e i debiti si
pagano.'* You cry for your sins and you pay your debts.''

''Other people's, too, sometimes.'' The murders weren't
my fault. But I'd groveled to keep a job that felt like penance,
every minute of it. And I couldn't seem to remember what
I'd ever liked about being a lawyer.

''The last time I heard my mother-in-law's voice she said
she wished she could kill me. For being a *puttana*.''

I'd spent enough time in North Beach to know that meant
harlot. ''I gather you left your first husband?''

She looked me in the eye, pencil-darkened brows raised.
''I had an affair. I was very young, I guess. I certainly cried
for that sin.''

''And you went to stay with Edward?''

"That was later." Hardly sprightly to begin with, she seemed to wilt completely. "If Friend doesn't make it— I should have gone with Edward."

"Edward wanted you to talk to me about Phil? So I could go talk to him?"

She blinked as if I'd suddenly spoken Greek to her. "Talk to Phil?"

"Yes. About your separation?"

"Maybe it's transference."

"What?"

"Maybe it's really Phil I don't feel safe without." She stared through rough-hewn French doors at a deck buzzing with sunlit bees. "All the things he rescued me from, years alone, phobias, tiny apartments." She rubbed her breastbone. "Sins to cry for and debts to pay."

"You left him recently?"

"At first, all he could think of was winning me; I was his project. I liked that."

I tried to imagine the feeling.

"Now Phil's project is the garden. When he's not working, he gardens. Once, before friends came over, he said, 'I want them to look at this garden and think, She's crazy to be unhappy.' " Her smile was somewhere between fond and contemptuous. "He was a conscientious objector to the Vietnam War—you'd never know it now. He never mentions it. Now he thinks he's political because he's on the boards of directors of theater ensembles, things like that. Local commissions. Things that look good on his résumé."

"So, um, do you want me to talk to him today? Or"—hopefully—"would you rather I didn't go?"

"Not that I'm a fan of ass-on-the-line convictions. I don't trust them. All those balls-to-the-wall people, they scare me."

"Yes." With feeling. "I know the type of people you

mean.'' I'd been browbeaten and maddened and bored by them at countless meetings.

"I don't know if it's a good idea to talk to Phil.'' She looked me in the eye as if I, not knowing her husband or her situation, could offer an opinion. "But maybe it's just fear— just hide and leave everything alone, blend in, all that stuff. I can't really keep doing that, not in this context. Have to think of the kids, for one thing. And Edward's so adamant— thinks it's so important. It's hard for me to know what's appropriate. Sometimes I don't care, sometimes I get . . .'' Tears sprang to her eyes. "I should have ridden with Friend.''

"If Edward thought that was a good idea, he'd have suggested it.'' Saint Edward the fucking Wise.

"And the kids, I should go get them.''

I eased to the edge of my chair. I'd told Edward I'd do this, and I would do it. But I hoped it wouldn't backfire on her. She didn't look like she could take much more. I knew that feeling too well to dismiss it cavalierly.

"What do you want to accomplish by having me talk to him?''

"Just ask Phil some questions.''

"Like what?''

She raised both hands in a gesture of helplessness. "Like if he's going to throw me to the wolves.''

"Throw you to the wolves? In what way?''

"He'll know.'' She rubbed a pale band of skin on her ring finger. "It's good that you're a woman. He goes into fight mode with men. He gets this surge of''—she shook her head—"I don't know what to call it. Testosterone. Adrenaline. Pure aggression.''

I thought of other litigators I'd met. "I know the type.''

"Maybe he'll hear your questions, instead of getting competitive right away.'' I noticed that her nails were short and her cuticles chewed. "Mention the kids. He can't take care of them—he's not home enough. So why hurt me? Why put me at risk?''

What did she think he was going to do? "You know, divorce is no-fault in this state. You might feel better having a family lawyer explain your rights to you.''

She crossed her forearms over her face.

I considered going to her. But I'd rather sit alone than be consoled. Lucky thing, too.

I looked at my watch. It was one thirty. I'd rolled into town at one, promising myself I'd roll back out at three. I could give it a little longer than that, I supposed. But I should get started.

I interrupted Rita's tears. "I'm not really sure of your agenda.'' God, I sounded like an L.A. lawyer. "But I'll talk to your husband, if you give me his address.''

She continued to cry, head bent. I noticed the part in her hair showed lighter roots, not gray or blond, maybe red.

"I'll stay till Edward gets back, if you want.''

But she shook her head. I had to wait a few minutes for her to choke out the address.

Only after I'd been lost an hour on mountain roads did I regret not waiting for her to calm down enough to give me directions.

14

I SAT IN PHILIP Delacort's backyard hammock while he planted pansies under an oak tree. He said he'd been expecting me, but I wasn't sure he'd been listening.

"Anyway," I concluded a rather strained monologue, "I owe this friend of your wife's a favor, and here I am."

He wiped dirt from his hands, shifting so that he faced me. Behind him, terraced strips of lawn were shaded by redwoods, firs and a few gnarled oaks. The hammock was in a patch of sun fluttering with tree shadows. We were in the foothills of the Santa Cruz Mountains. The air smelled like pine needles and damp grass.

Delacort said, "She couldn't talk to me herself? What have I ever done to her? What does she think I'm going to do now?" He spoke with the cheerful, open countenance of a man discussing pansy beds. "Look around, this was her life with me. I never did anything but support her." A slight frown behind lightly tinted shades. "She's the one who took off."

"I don't know why she sent me to talk to you." And I felt like a creep discussing her. Damn Edward Hershey anyway. "I only just met her for the first time. Like I said, this is a favor for a mutual friend. But"—I'd known too many litigators to trust Delacort's surface pleasantness—"she's expressed a fear that you'll throw her to the wolves."

His face went tight, as if every muscle had contracted. "That's stupid."

"It is?"

"Obviously I know her address. She's living with—" He scowled, stabbing his trowel into the dirt. "I've left her alone, haven't I?"

I rocked in the hammock, thinking how good it felt to have a faceful of sun. Peaceful, secluded—I could see why Rita Delacort had pangs about leaving.

"So you're not planning to get back at her?" Might as well come out with it. It was too personal and offensive a question to hedge.

He studied me for a moment. "What do you mean?"

"Hardball property negotiations, custody disputes." I thought about it, trying to cover the bases. "Revenge, personal or financial or through the children."

He stared at his grimy hands. A filtered ray of sunlight caught lines of tension in his forehead, a throbbing tic beside one eye. "Would you expect me to admit any of that to you? To her?"

"No."

"Then what good is my answer?"

"Getting it—and I guess trying to assess whether it's true— is part of the favor I'm doing."

"All right." He ran a finger under the lace of his well-worn Top-Sider. His shorts gapped at the thigh, offering a glimpse of blue cotton briefs. "The answer is no, I'm a saint. Time I'd have spent with my family, I'll spend out here gardening. And as for my wife—yes, she can have custody of the kids, she can have her share of the property. However Rita wants things, she shall have them."

An ancient curse.

Like libido. I stopped ogling the colored briefs, and took my midlife crisis back on the road.

15

HE DIDN'T SEEM worse than most lawyers," I said generously. "If he has a plan, it's probably something subtle. He doesn't seem interested in the obvious things—property, custody."

Rita Delacort was very pale, regarding me with glazed wide eyes. She was afraid of something, probably something in particular. Edward stood behind her, hands on her shoulders. I noticed his fingers tightening.

"He won't do anything crazy, Rita." His voice was heavy with meaning. Definitely something in particular.

"Well, he says he won't hassle you about custody." I shrugged. "I don't know the man at all, but he seemed to mean it. He might be good at seeming to mean things, though."

"He is," Rita said through clenched teeth.

"That," I added dryly, "is the problem with sending over someone who doesn't know him. I have no idea what to tell you. He wasn't particularly forthcoming. I don't see why he should have been, under the circumstances."

"He never is. I'm not sure there's anything under that calmness of his, I'm not sure there's any emotion left. Just strategy."

She'd lived with him eight years and had two kids by him. It gave me chills that she could talk about him that way.

I looked at Edward. What if I'd stayed with him all these years? Would I have reached a point where I could talk about him like a snake expert discussing venom? Would he have become an object in my life, a landmark to be discussed without warmth?

I remembered a conversation I'd had with Don Surgelato once. He'd told me about his (then) ex-wife, how repugnant he'd found her "cocktail-party charm."

Maybe all married people find each other repugnant. Maybe that's part of the package. Maybe it's the other stuff— the single-life stresses Surgelato described, the fears Rita now experienced—that keeps couples together. And right they are to stay together. It's killingly lonely out here. Better to coil up with a snake or party with a brittle princess. Company is company.

Edward, still standing behind her, began massaging Rita's shoulders. "You'll be okay," he said. "He stills cares about you."

From behind a closed door, a faint mewling became audible. Then loud.

"Well," she said. "So much for nap time."

Edward said, "Stay put. I'll take care of them."

She touched her cheek to his hand. "Edward." She spoke the name with reverence.

The mewling turned into a cry of "Mommy!"

She watched Edward leave the living room. "Not once in the years since they were born has Philip gone in to them. Not even once." She turned to me. "You never know how someone will be in a role until they're in it, I guess."

Two golden-haired children, one a toddler, one a pre-schooler, erupted into the room. Close on their heels, Edward called, "Whoa. I told you—"

Rita Delacort opened her arms and the children jumped her, filling the room with noise and child smells—graham crackers, diapers, powder. As she hugged them, her eyes suddenly scrunched, her cheeks knotted, her lips pulled away from her teeth.

She clutched the children like stuffed bears. Edward looked about a hundred years old, watching her.

With Philip Delacort momentarily out of my consciousness, I remembered to ask about the dog.

Standing over Rita, Edward said, "He'll be fine." But he looked at me and shook his head, glancing down. I wasn't sure who he was protecting from the truth, Rita or her children.

Ironically enough, I remember being grateful that Rita Delacort's problems weren't mine.

16

MONDAY MORNING, SLIGHTLY hung over, I slogged through a hundred-page transcript of a Social Security hearing. I was looking for a way to overturn the denial of benefits to a multiple sclerosis sufferer. George sat opposite me at his desk, flipping through appellate court cases in a futile effort to uphold an "implied" Miranda warning. We were like two little law students working on our moot court briefs. That was okay for George—he was just out of law school, after all. But I was supposed to be a real grown-up lawyer now.

My phone buzzed—a summons from the judge.

He was sitting at his desk, his posture stiff, his face as stonily grim as an eagle's. There was a man sitting opposite him, his back to the door. I glanced at the man without much curiosity. A lawyer, definitely. I could tell by the perfect haircut and the expensive suit worn with obvious ease.

I hesitated a moment before approaching the judge's desk. His expression was less than welcoming as he watched me walk the twenty feet to his desk. Just watched; didn't say anything.

When I reached the companion chair to the one occupied by the perfect haircut, I finally understood.

The man looked at me. And I felt as apprehensive as a kid in the principal's office.

It was Philip Delacort.

The judge said, "You know Mr. Delacort."

"Yes." What came out of my mouth didn't sound like "yes," exactly, but the judge got the drift.

"Sit down. Mr. Delacort has been telling me about your conversation with him on Saturday."

I glanced at Delacort. He looked damned pleased with himself.

I didn't say anything. Had I done something improper? I must have, for Judge Shanna to look so grim.

"You are perhaps not aware," the judge said, "that Mr. Delacort has a case before us?"

"A case?" A Santa Cruz attorney? Up here?

"A case," the judge repeated. "Upon which George has devoted some hours over the last few weeks."

"But I didn't know—I don't understand . . . A Santa Cruz lawyer—"

Delacort interrupted. "My practice is in San Jose and San Francisco. In this instance, I represent a Silicon Valley client who—"

"But Edward Hershey told me . . ." Nothing. Nothing about Delacort's practice; only that he was a big shot in Santa Cruz.

"You must realize that ex parte"—private—"communications in a situation like this . . .'' The judge ran a hand over his stiff auburn waves.

I'd told Hershey I was working for Judge Shanna, and he'd asked me to do him a favor. He asked me *after* learning I was clerking for the judge.

After. He'd set this up. Either with Delacort or against Delacort, he'd set this up.

"I'm afraid Mr. Delacort is quite rightly dismayed."

"I'm sorry. I didn't know."

If only I hadn't run into Edward outside my parents' flat.

But no, it was too coincidental. I remembered Mother's flashes of guilt and confusion that evening. He'd asked her to arrange the meeting; how else could he have known I'd be there?

With my parents' collusion, the bastard had lain in wait for me.

I stared at Delacort, stunned.

Delacort said, "I had no idea you were the judge's clerk, or I'd have insisted you leave." He shrugged, his even features pleasant and unmoved. "As it is, I can't help but feel my case has been compromised."

"What case? What's the case about?"

"A securities fraud matter," the judge said curtly. "George can fill you in. In the meantime, you don't deny that you visited Mr. Delacort at his home?"

Securities fraud. Judge Shanna was the most liberal judge on the federal court bench; therefore the most likely to come down hard on white-collar crime.

"No, I don't deny it. But I was doing a friend a favor. Speaking to Mr. Delacort on behalf of his wife. Nothing to do with a securities fraud case." I felt as if my head would come spinning off; too much blood to the brain, too many synapses firing. Why had Edward done this? Why had my mother helped? "I didn't know he had a case before you. In fact, I was given to understand that Mr. Delacort was a Santa Cruz lawyer.'' A small-town lawyer, not a lawyer with a federal practice.

Delacort shook his head incredulously.

The judge's lips pursed. He turned to Delacort. ''I accept, and must insist that you accept, Ms. Jansson's assurance that she acted in ignorance and good faith.'' He sounded like he was reading from a script.

Delacort responded like a chameleon, changing expression to suit the judicial climate. ''Absolutely, Your Honor. I have no basis at this point for any accusation against Ms. Jansson. But the fact remains . . .''

The judge rose, five-feet-five of dignity. ''Thank you for bringing this to my attention, Mr. Delacort. We'll be in touch with your office.''

Delacort rose. His face was expressionless except for a pinched corner of the mouth and a wary sparkle of the eye. He extended his hand across the desk.

The men shook hands briefly. Delacort said, ''Fine, Your Honor. I look forward to hearing from you.''

Then he turned to me, regarding me with what seemed to be unshaded curiosity. He didn't say anything, didn't try to shake my hand. He looked at me a little longer than was strictly polite; a lot longer than I wanted to be looked at. Then he left.

The judge sat wearily. ''Well, this is rather unfortunate.''

''I don't understand. I was asked by a friend to intercede for Delacort's wife. She left him and she wanted to know what he was planning to do. She was afraid to talk—'' I felt tears spring to my eyes. ''I don't understand what just happened. I don't understand this.''

''Mr. Delacort has requested I disqualify myself from hearing his case.''

''But I didn't compromise the case. I really didn't.''

"In all likelihood it will be an eighteen-month, two-year case. If I don't disqualify myself, there is a risk that, at the end of that time, Delacort will take his adverse ruling and appeal it based on this incident. Based on the apparent impropriety of receiving a visit at home from my clerk." His nostrils flared. His eyes glinted with something that to me looked like pure hatred. Of the way I'd fucked up. Maybe of me.

"I don't understand," I repeated weakly. "Why did Hershey do this?" I stood, side-stepping the chair. Why did Mother help him?

I began backing out of chambers. The room swayed as if it were cupped in a giant hammock.

"I don't get this," I heard myself say. "I'm sorry, I just don't get this." Why were they fucking with me?

The judge sat there, presumably watching me, maybe even saying something to me. He was a blur, the room was a blur. I couldn't see him, not really, just the shape of his anger. I couldn't hear him, just the conch-shell roar of disapproval in my ears.

I backed up, apologizing still. And telling him over and over again that I didn't get it.

The last thing I said before I walked out the door was "I quit."

17

I WAS ON THE ledge of a building. Every inch of my skin screamed with cold. My clothes were like sheets of ice, the night wind blinded me, my feet were blocks of lead on a shallow foothold. I pressed my cheek to the rough concrete and tried to burrow my fingernails into the wall.

I heard gunfire, blasts so loud they might have come from cannons. Around me, concrete exploded. Beside my cheek, hand and leg, the wall fragmented into huge holes. The ledge beneath my feet shattered into clouds of dust, filling my nose, my mouth, choking me as my nails clung to the concrete.

Jump, an internal voice commanded. *Jump and don't find out and don't ever know.*

My fingers snaked deeper into the friable concrete, leaving

streaks of blood; and I hung there, my feet scrabbling for some bit of toehold.

Jump and don't find out and don't ever know.

It was an external voice now, as large and quadraphonic as the voice of God.

Jump. Don't find out. Don't know.

I felt my grip loosen and I thought, Okay, then, I'll fall, just fall. Instead, a jet of wind buoyed me, tumbling and battering me across the face of the building. The wind scraped me over concrete to the window of Julian Warneke's office. I was pinned there, flailing to push away, push off, go down.

But it was no use. Through a window I could see—I was forced to watch—Julian Warneke's killer raise and aim a gun. A long gun, its barrel as broad as a lead pipe.

A face slid in and out of focus: Julian Warneke's killer, sometimes; a law school friend, sometimes; a former co-worker. All three were killers. A voice in the wind said, *Hey, hey, LBJ, how many kids did you kill today?*

And I woke up gasping. Sweating.

As usual.

My fingers clutched the pillow, my feet scrambled the blankets.

And I felt myself falling. At the moment of wakening, I felt a swirling, nauseating vertigo, as if I were falling.

And worse: I felt the terror of standing on the ledge outside Julian Warneke's office. In full, exaggerated detail, I stood on that ledge again while Julian's killer prowled inside, gun in hand.

Something I never let myself think about. Never. Whatever my therapist might urge.

Because I don't need reminding that the world is a scary place. I don't need reminding that you trust a friend at your own peril.

I slid out of bed. My God, I needed a joint. I needed to take the grim chill off reality.

Why did I quit, anyway? Why throw out the medicine when the symptoms persist?

I did the best I could with a bottle of white wine. Yuppie morphine.

18

THE WAY I felt Tuesday morning, I knew I wouldn't be drinking again any time soon. I felt dehydrated, stiff-jointed, nauseous. My eyes burned and my temples seemed to be imploding. I'd gotten brutally sick.

I took a walk to Stanyan Street, to a cramped little walkup I'd visited often in the last twenty years. I bought some green and leafy comfort. If I was going to medicate, why not do it with my drug of choice?

I walked down the Panhandle to Haight Street.

There was a fair-sized crowd there, students in wire-frames and baggy sweaters, time-warp hippies in army jackets and fringed mocs, punks and gays with bleached hair and black leather, middle-aged beats with alert faces and paperbacks sticking out of their back pockets. I was standing in front of

Pipedreams, the ghost of a great old head shop, listening to a street musician strum "Rainy Day Woman" and wail on his harmonica. Pipedreams had its black lights on; psychedelic posters glowed in the windows.

A voice behind me said, "Willa June."

Only one person calls me that. I turned around to face my mother.

She was wearing old jeans, grocery store shoes and a sweater so stretched it could have passed for a tunic. Anything fancier would have been a waste of money she could have donated to a worthy cause. Measured by what she gave instead of what she consumed, she was worth a hundred of the elegant lawyers at Wailes, Roth.

I embraced her. She was momentarily stiff in my arms, then she clutched me with an awkward excess of emotion. When I pulled away, her eyes were bright.

I didn't bother with, How are you. I said, "Did you arrange to have Edward Hershey in front of your house when I got there?"

She flinched. "No."

I watched her wrap her arms around herself, tuck her chin down, look away. I was reminded of an anemone closing up.

She disliked being the object of (nonpolitical) ire, reacted with the rebellious-child demeanor of a strict upbringing. If I challenged her lie, she'd stick to it even more stubbornly.

And my guess, after a long night of deliberation, was that she'd been matchmaking. She'd always liked Hershey, certainly liked him better than any of my recent, politically incorrect boyfriends. If he asked her to help arrange an "accidental" meeting, she'd bathe it in romantic connotations.

I hoped that was all there was to it.

"You're out shopping?"

She shook her head, stepping back to let a band of street people jostle past. "Out for a walk."

"Me, too. A lot of changes here."

When I left for L.A., Haight Street was a chichi market-place of expensive cookware and stylish boutiques. Now, everywhere I looked there were echoes of 1968. Head shops that sold everything but actual paraphernalia, underground comics stores, hologram galleries, honest little stores selling staples instead of luxuries. Even the people on the street had changed, from overweight professionals in expensive running shoes to students and neighbors. Sometime last year Haight Street had risen from its own ashes.

Mother gestured impatiently at the head shop behind me. "I hate to see this nostalgia. It's so pointless in this political context."

"Maybe it's a way of burrowing in. Keeping a minority culture alive."

She looked a little pained, glancing at my button-down blouse, at the Coach bag slung over my shoulder. "Not alive. Embalmed."

Embalmed. A sarcophagal display for former hippies in their broadcloth and new leather.

"Well, it's better than last year, with all that yuppie junk."

Her blue eyes winced into a trouble frown. "I guess the yuppies have all the junk they need by now. Now they want to pretend they used to be part of something, used to believe in something." She sounded more deflated than outraged. "As if that's a substitute for believing in something now."

"Such as what?" What philosophy, political or personal, could survive twenty years of scrutiny and perspective?

"Such as what we always believed!"

"Oh, Mother. We believed that stuff as hard as we could and where did it get us? The eighties turned into the fifties. Why not be honest about it?"

"Why not be cynical about it, you mean." She drew back, stood straighter; regarded me across a wide chasm of ideology. "It's easier to focus on the trappings, I suppose—to think about it in terms of beads and posters versus I don't know what—whatever it is you people like now—cars and clothes, whatever."

You people. You yuppies. Ouch.

"I should get going."

There was a glint of pain in her eyes. "You should come to dinner, Willa June."

"Soon."

"Your father and I, we were just talking about how much we miss our family dinners." She was beginning to sound wistful. "When you used to sleep over."

I kissed her cheek. She smelled like incense and old sweater. Like a mother's embrace when you're a kid.

You yuppies. I walked away.

19

I SPENT THE rest of the afternoon alternating joints and naps, kiting on regret.

I'd done so much for my résumé. Years of college—years of cerebral bullshit and predatory debt. Law school, the bar exam. And lately, suffering in smoggy exile, loathing every minute of a full year of my life. I'd finally become impressive on paper, if in no other venue. And damn, I'd thrown it away.

I considered calling my therapist in L.A. But it struck me that I wasn't any happier or any saner this year than last. Maybe being in therapy is like scratching mosquito bites. Maybe thinking about your problems just inflames them, spreads them to clean tissue until everything itches.

At about four o'clock, my doorbell rang. I was in the

living room, comfortably high, thinking the hell with it, so what if I'd behaved unprofessionally? If I didn't care (the weak point in my argument), why should anyone else care?

I flung open the door and found George McLeod standing in the hall. George, looking lean and grouchy in a white shirt and blue tie, suit jacket slung over his arm. His chin was knotted so that his clipped beard bristled, his brows were comically lowered, his face and thinning hair were damp with sweat. He sniffed a few times to let me know he smelled and disapproved of my last joint.

"The judge sent me," he announced, as if I'd roll out a red carpet. When I didn't, he snapped, "Can I please come in?"

I tried out my voice. "Sure." Smoking had given it a Janis Joplin rasp. I cleared my throat, stepping aside to let him enter.

He looked around the living room, shaking his head. Expensive new furniture hadn't made me a tidier person, I'm afraid.

I dropped into the sofa, letting him decide which chair to clear of sweatclothes.

"We've been phoning you all day," he accused me, sitting on dingy Stanford sweats.

"I unplugged the phone."

"What are you doing, anyway?"

"Hanging out."

"Are you nuts or what? How about work? What are you—what are you—?" Words failed him.

"I'm hanging out," I repeated. "I quit, that's what about work. So I'm hanging out."

George shook his head, not slightly, but widely and slowly, apparently in lieu of harsh criticism. "The judge figured you were upset, he didn't figure you meant it. We expected you back today. We've been calling you. I mean, you've got to—

You should come back with me right now. I think you can still—'' He shook his head again.

''No.''

He leaned forward in his chair. ''You can't quit a clerk-ship!''

Yesterday morning, I'd have agreed with him. ''If you check the reality meter, you'll find that I did quit. Whether I can or not, I did.'' Embers of shame kindled. ''Why did the judge send you?''

''To find out what's going on.''

I tried to spare myself a mental replay of the scene in chambers. Didn't succeed. Damn.

Damn.

''You really quit?'' George's tone was impatient, angry. His cheeks were pink with exasperation. ''It's stupid to quit. It's not that big a deal. In a way it is, but in a way it isn't. I mean, ex parte communications aren't that uncommon.''

''Lawyers are ex parte animals.''

''I didn't put that many hours into the case—we've only had it a few weeks. It's not like we're in trial. Besides, you didn't know about it, the judge said.'' George tilted his head, watching me as if to measure my veracity. ''You didn't know?''

I was looking at George, thinking how long it had been since anyone had come to my apartment, here or in L.A. I looked at George and took unexpected comfort in his presence. Even if he did like to argue. Even if he was a Republican.

But then, I'd gotten equally sentimental about Edward Hershey, hadn't I? I'd started thinking he was a friend of mine; that just because we had a little history, maybe I could trust him.

''I didn't know. I thought I was interceding with Delacort for his wife. As a favor to a—an acquaintance.''

"Did the acquaintance know you worked for the judge?"

I nodded. "You met him the other morning at the office. Edward Hershey. A private detective in Santa Cruz."

George scowled. "Does he do any pretrial investigation?"

"I assume so."

"Well, Delacort got the securities case sent up for reassignment. The cases are initially assigned by the computer. Randomly. But they get reassigned by the presiding judge." He smoothed his mustache thoughtfully. "Judge Rondi's the temporary P.J. since Bendix retired, until they appoint a new one."

Rondi. The fascist who'd sent me to jail.

"Seniority," George continued. "Rondi's an Eisenhower appointee, did you know that? Anyway, Judge Shanna's in a snit because Rondi decided to keep the case for himself. Rondi doesn't believe in white-collar crime. He calls it 'creative business management'—wrote a law review article about it a couple of years ago." More mustache-stroking. "Actually, I agree with Rondi, but it's problematic the way this came up. Considering Shanna's reputation for nailing white-collar criminals." Stroke, stroke. "Delacort was awfully lucky to get the case reassigned."

"Either that or he paid Edward Hershey to arrange it."

George's face twisted into something between a pucker and a grimace. "By duping a judge's clerk? How would you even frame the accusation?"

"Interfering with a pending lawsuit?"

"No, the suit's going forward."

Damn them. Rondi and Hershey. I'd despised them since 1971. What kind of malicious irony had put them back into my life? Both of them. At the same time.

"Tell me more about Delacort's case," I commanded. Maybe it would teach me something about my kismet.

But I should have known it had nothing to do with kismet.

And I should have known I was too stoned to follow an explanation of securities fraud, however karmically significant I supposed it to be. I gathered the case had something to do with corporations "floating bonds" based on their reputations rather than their assets, about making that sound okay to investors. George launched into a diatribe about corporate documentation, getting very red of face.

"I told Judge Shanna there was nothing technically wrong with the transaction, that it turned on whether or not there was an intention to defraud. Or looking at it another way, a duty to point out that the bonds were basically junk. A staggering debt load for the company and very hard to trade. Plaintiffs say they thought, based on various representations, that they were buying a kind of stock, even if it was billed as a debt instrument."

I tried to concentrate on George's explanation, but I was stoned. When you're stoned, random thoughts are given as much weight as matters at hand. I thought as much about George's tie (why did lawyers switch from red ties to blue ties after Bush was elected?) as I did his words. I thought about corporate law in general; regulations, contract clauses, endless dilatory motions. Lawyers who talked about their purchases, their vacations, their workouts. God deliver me.

I tried to phase back in. "Delacort is the corporation's lawyer?"

George nodded. "He works for the San Jose office of a big L.A. firm. L.A. did the documentation. Delacort's in the corporate litigation department. He specializes in Silicon Valley high-tech trials."

Yes, it made sense. Santa Cruz lacked the industry and corporations necessary to support a wealthy lawyer. San Jose, on the other hand, was a banquet table of techno-business. Delacort's fine house screamed commuter-lawyer; only I hadn't bothered to think about it. I'd been too busy thinking about love gone awry.

"You know what I think?" George squirmed in his chair. "I think Rondi will throw the case out on Delacort's summary judgment motion. A few more days and I'll bet the case is out of court."

"Who represents the plaintiffs? Who *are* the plaintiffs?"

"Who aren't? It's an investors' class action."

"Who's the lawyer for the class?"

George looked mildly surprised. "I thought you knew—you're so interested in him. Harry Prough."

Kurt Vonnegut says there are people who periodically meander through your life, people you rediscover with surprise and chagrin, like a recurring rash. He says they're part of your cosmic team, your "karass." Hershey, Rondi—they'd been pains in the karass for a long time. Now it seemed Harry Prough had joined the ranks.

George glanced at his watch. I expected him to say he needed to get going. I expected him to demand an answer to take back to the judge. Instead he said, "Have you had dinner?"

I wasn't sure I'd heard him right.

He followed up with, "Are you okay? I didn't mean to come over here and, you know, come down on you if you're upset."

"I'm okay."

He didn't look convinced. "Let's go eat," he repeated. "Come on. I'd really like to have dinner with you."

I stood hastily and walked toward the bedroom—that was the only way I could think of to turn my back on him. I then said the only thing I could say consistent with that behavior. I said, "I'll get a sweater."

I closed the bedroom door behind me and let myself get

misty-eyed. I don't know why—dinner invitations don't usually do that to me.

George and I bought hoagies and ate them in Buena Vista Park. We talked about law school and movies. The summer fog had rolled in with a vengeance; we had the park to ourselves. Things didn't seem so bad.

"The judge assumes you're sick or shaken up or something. He expects you back," George repeated. "So you'll have to call him if you mean it about quitting."

"But I told him yesterday—"

"Or you could do what he expects you to do." He waved aside a panhandler. "Show up tomorrow. Keep things simple."

Simple. Yes, employment did keep things simple. It narrowed the scope of midlife crisis. It paid the Macy's bills.

"Maybe." Alternatively, I could spend my days drinking wine and trying to raise my nausea threshold. "Yeah, okay."

George smiled, lightly punching my arm. Then he reddened. I wished my therapist could see it: someone more uncomfortable with small intimacies than I am.

I was home by six thirty. I paced a while, running my fingers through my hair. I'd committed myself to getting it together by morning, to going back to my job and facing the judge and putting my life back together.

I had to detox. I drove to the Golden Gate Bridge with what remained of my brand-new lid of pot.

I stood on the bay side of the bridge shivering in the knife-slice wind, my fingers curled around the Baggie of pot in my pocket. I looked past Alcatraz and Angel Island at the Marina, mottled with black gaps like missing pieces in a jigsaw puzzle. The house Julian Warneke bequeathed to my mother was gone; collapsed in the earthquake I'd missed. Mother's "safe house" for Salvadorans with expired visas was now a piece of prime real estate she couldn't afford to build on but

was too sentimental to sell. Like the sixties; we didn't know
how to replace it but we couldn't seem to let go of it.

It was a gray-sky evening, the bay dark and choppy, dotted
with tilted sailboats.

I looked straight down, my hand still in my pocket. I didn't
know if I could survive without pot, if I could survive without its numbing vagueness and impairment. Besides, tossing
my pot away hadn't helped much last time. I'd fucked things
up quite efficiently without it.

I left the Baggie in my pocket, and put both hands on the
red steel bridge rail. It was slick and cold under my hands.
It vibrated with the rush of traffic, thousands of tons of metal.
I looked down at the water, deep gray-green in the evening
overcast. The moving shades of gray were hypnotic, impel-
ling.

I could carry my pot right off the bridge. Jump, as I'd
wanted to do in my dream.

Maybe that's why I'd come to the bridge. Maybe I'd come
to jump.

I could have flushed my pot down the toilet. Maybe I'd
really come here to jump.

Jump and don't find out and don't ever know: just like in
my dream. Except that it was too late—I knew who killed
Julian Warneke.

I knew—I just didn't want to think about it.

Don't find out and don't ever know. Don't find out what?
Whether I could handle a career? Keep my personal life together? Trust anyone?

I stared at the water a long time. My hands went numb on
the icy rail.

I didn't jump. Neither did my pot.

20

I WAS LATE for work Wednesday morning. There was a long line at the lobby metal detectors, but the guard recognized me and waved me behind him.

The eighteenth-floor corridor was austere and cool, deserted except for an occasional clerk. Two floors above me, reporters pounded computer keys and burned up phone lines. Two floors below, lawyers flipped pages and yawned in the law library. But here there was an atmosphere of activity locked deep within the warren, hidden behind massive doors and defended by intercoms and buzzers.

As long as I could keep it together and act like a lawyer (a practical if not noble aspiration), I'd be okay. I rounded a corner and almost collided with a tiny man in a black suit. I backed away, beginning my instinctive apology, when I realized who he was. The Honorable Manolo M. Rondi, prune-faced fascist and author of the most traumatic two months of my life.

We stared at one another warily. The memory clearly reflected in his eyes that two years ago, I'd genteelly blackmailed him into a suspended sentence for an activist client of mine. Our cards had never been on the table: I hadn't wanted to be disbarred for suborning a judge and he hadn't wanted to admit his unjudicial conduct. A few elliptical references had been enough—enough to get my client off the hook, and refuel Rondi's hatred of me.

We stood there for a shocked moment. Then he looked up and down the corridor, apparently checking if we were alone. He bent slightly—almost conspiratorially—closer. Through lips glued to his teeth he whispered, "I don't know what you think you're up to with this securities case, I really don't know. But I'll find out, I'll tell you that right now. Because Mike Shanna doesn't bow out of a case for no good reason." He nodded for emphasis, not a strand of black hair escaping its pomade. "You did more than Mike's telling. That's clear."

He took a step backward, making an exaggerated arc around me as he walked away. I stood there a while, trying not to inhale the lingering garlic of his breath.

When I got to the office I shared with George, I found a phone message on my desk.

From Edward. The slip of paper bore no message, just his office number.

Did he think I was still a naïve little nineteen-year-old, willing to believe fence-mending lies?

I crumpled the square of paper and launched it at the office door. Just in time for the door to swing open.

The balled-up message bounced off George McLeod's chest and skittered across the tight weave of carpet. George looked down, one eyebrow raised. Then he bent to retrieve the paper, uncrumpling it as he straightened.

He read it, closing the door behind him. He stuck out his lower lip, something bearded men should never do. He walked thoughtfully to his desk.

He sat with the message spread on his blotter, looking at me.

"Did you know I'm divorced?"

"No." I thought of him as a kid. Just out of law school. Probably went straight to college after high school—not like me, gypsying away most of a decade before the charm of "life experience" was eclipsed by the paltriness of minimum wage. George probably went straight through college and law school, no break. He was now a mature twentysomething to my immature thirtysomething.

"My wife kept coming in late, really late, with preposterous explanations." He shrugged. "I debated about believing her—it had obvious advantages; I happened to love her very much. But. But but but."

I waited for the punch line. When he didn't supply one, I guessed, "It turned out she'd been telling the truth?"

He looked surprised. "How would I know? I divorced her."

"I don't get your point."

"I don't either." A long sigh. "I keep wondering if I'll ever meet anybody else."

I watched him smooth the phone message with his fist.

"I think," he added, "that you trust people for your own sake, not theirs."

"That's not the party line, George. The whole point of being a lawyer is to keep your eyes open. Know the facts so you can manipulate them."

He continued smoothing the message slip, absently gazing down at it.

Finally he met my eye. "I graduated from law school in January, you know that. But you think I did an accelerated program and got out in two and half years, don't you?" He barely paused; no answer was required. "Actually, I took the last half of my second year off. My divorce was that hard."

I was interested in the information, but I wasn't sure of his point. Maybe he wasn't, either. He opened a file folder and began spreading documents over his desktop.

I waited for him to say more, but he didn't.

21

MY THERAPIST USED to talk about trust, making it sound like a philosophy; the choice, apparently, of self-actualized folk. My parents, he'd pointed out, had "abandoned" me by going off to jail; and now I expected everyone to abandon me. Especially since some people—friends, I'd thought—had tried to abandon me right into my grave.

Yes, my therapist was aware that even paranoids have real enemies—that I myself am a three-time winner of the Miss Justified Paranoia crown. But, he'd countered, it's "personally destructive" to go through life anticipating betrayal. As a matter of philosophical style, it makes sense to move toward a "generalized, if cautious" trust. Universal distrust could only keep me "defended and locked in."

I thought about my year in L.A.—holed up every night

smoking pot—and I suspected my therapist was right. Small comfort: not only was I politically incorrect, I was psychologically incorrect.

I supposed I'd feel better about life if I could take the leap of faith required to believe that my friends (whoever they might be) were straight with me.

But I wasn't good at leaps of faith. Every time I took one, I fell into the chasm.

So I devised a compromise: If I could figure out who was lying about what, then by process of elimination I could figure out whom to trust. After a little cautious prescreening, I would take the leap. I would weed out the liars, and give everyone else keys to my no-longer-cynical heart. I would put Leo Buscaglia to shame.

Saturday morning, I drove down to Santa Cruz.

I found Edward Hershey in his driveway, strapping a kayak to the roof of his Jeep. When my car rolled in behind his, he looked disconcerted, to say the least.

He also looked like he'd been kicked around the block. His lips were swollen and one eyebrow had been stitched. His cheeks and jaw were the color of bad veal.

Before I could ask him about it, he said, "I didn't know Delacort had a case with Shanna. Honest to God." He backed away when I climbed out of my car, his hands extended palms out.

"What happened to you?"

He reached reflexively toward his face. "Minor ambush. No biggie."

Curiosity overcame me. "Seriously, what happened?"

"Break-in, here, middle of Sunday night."

"You surprised a burglar?"

He gave the rope a tug, securing the kayak to the Jeep roof. "Someone appeared in my bedroom. Smacked me a few times and left. Like I said, no biggie."

"What about Rita?"

"Wasn't here." He sighed. "Wish I could say you should see the other guy. But I didn't even get a look at him. It was pow, pow, good-bye."

"You don't know who it was? He didn't take anything?"

"No." He scowled at the length of rope in his hand, gave it another tug. Fiddled with it a few more minutes, ignoring me.

Despite his obvious infirmity, I remained hostile; hot in my T-shirt and jeans, hazy from last night's pot. "I don't believe you about Delacort. You knew. You set the situation up."

"Fuck you." He scratched his thigh where his baggies ended. "I've got better things to do than stand here and get hassled by you today."

I wondered how many more bruises would fit on that smug face. "If you want to carry your kayak on your head, fine. But I'm not unblocking your car. Not till you prove you don't work for Delacort."

He turned slowly to face me. The improved view of the damage made me wince. For a minute, we just stood there.

"This is so fucking like you, Willa. How many times have I apologized about the herpes so far? Six hundred times, do you think? What more do you want from me?" He collapsed dramatically onto bent knees, clutching his hands to his heart. "Forgive me, mea culpa, I am so motherfucking sorry. Okay?"

"This isn't about the herpes." I had a more recent betrayal to lay at his door, as he well knew. "And you're slime to bring it up. You're saying I don't have a right to be angry that you lied to me about Delacort. You're saying my anger comes from something else—something, by the way, that you have never apologized for. Not six hundred times or ever.

Down on your fucking knees—you're not apologizing to me. You're putting on a show—and a hell of an insincere one."

"Mea culpa, mea fucking culpa. Six hundred and two." He stood. "When did I lie to you about Delacort?"

"When you told me he was a Santa Cruz attorney."

"I never said that. I might have said he *lives* in Santa Cruz. I never said he works here."

I tried to remember Edward's exact words. "It doesn't matter—you knew the impression you left."

"Oh, did I?" He touched his ribs as if they ached. "How am I supposed to know what you'll— Hell, every time I see you, you go batshit about something that happened nineteen years ago. Every time I try to be friendly, you practically cut off my dick. How am I supposed to have a clue what you'll think? Except that you'll jump to some terrible conclusion about me."

I steadied myself by leaning against my car. "I know lawyers like you, Edward. You ask them about X and they get angry about Y—to deflect you into another argument, one you're not prepared for and can't win." I might be paranoid, damn it, but it didn't make me wrong. It didn't make me stupid. It didn't give Edward fucking Hershey the right to patronize me. "You're working for Delacort, not his wife."

"What's the point of this? You didn't lose your job, did you?"

"My job's not the issue." I could almost feel the cold steel of the Golden Gate Bridge under my hands. No way to explain to Hershey how I'd felt. "The point is, I thought you were being straight with me. I'm sure Rita Delacort thinks you're being straight with her. And you're just using us to help Delacort win a case. Using us—selling out your friends."

He shook his battered head, turning away. But he didn't deny it.

22

It was a long shot. I was surprised to find Rita Delacort at her husband's house.

She opened the door to me calmly, almost languidly. "The kids aren't quite asleep. Do you mind if we sit out here?"

"Fine." Her cedar porch was bigger than my living room and more expensively furnished. I sat on a deep-cushioned redwood chair while she took the matching loveseat. Around us, trees creaked and leaves fluttered.

She said, "Edward phoned. He thought you might be coming up here."

"Are you back together with your husband?"

"I don't know." She seemed poured onto the cushion, pale under her freckles, skinny arms and legs unselfconsciously splayed. She looked like I felt. ''Whether I am or not, I should be.''

I remembered Delacort's confident stride as he left Judge Shanna's office. His perfect haircut. His wonderful house. The women at Wailes, Roth would kill for a husband like him.

''What's funny,'' she continued, ''is how much my first mother-in-law would like Phil. For being *somebody*. A big shot.''

''Your first husband wasn't?''

''Hardly. We got married at nineteen.'' The memory seemed to drain her of remaining energy and color. ''Nineteen. Madly, madly in love with someone a little crazy. Even more in love with his mother. She was so Italian.'' A weak smile. ''My parents are assimilated Irish. Republican. Presbyterian. Copper aspic molds on the wall.''

I used to watch television occasionally, see that kind of family. In rooms stacked with antidraft fliers, crowded with bitter veterans against the war, worrying about making someone's bail, I'd assumed those families were media constructs. It always surprised me to learn people had actually lived unglamorized versions of *The Donna Reed Show*.

''Now my mother-in-law, she was really something. She'd led such a hard life, such an operatic life—brothers dying in the war, hometown bombed, immigrating with two small children, almost going to jail for refusing to let them check her pubic hair at Ellis Island.'' She met my eye, seemed to need reassurance that I understood. ''*My* parents, they don't show emotion. They save their animation for parties. They put on this relentless, almost predatory charm. Phil does that sometimes. I hate it.''

''Did your first marriage last long?''

''No.'' She wiped a sudden layer of moisture from her cheeks. ''Everyone saying how unhip monogamy was, and

all those teenage hormones, and I think I even believed T—
my husband—wouldn't mind too much, he was so vanguard.
But mostly, I think it was just Edward, who he was and how
that fit with who I was.''

Edward. Mr. fucking Right.

"The worst of it," she continued, "was how completely
wrong I was. How I kept looking at things in black and white.
Glamorizing.''

"Glamorizing Edward?" I felt a twinge. Because she
might have been the one in Boston? A lot of years had passed.
On the other hand, I hadn't loved many men.

"No. My mother-in-law. That culture. Otherness in general.'' She pushed damp hair off her face, sitting up suddenly. She leaned closer. "She phoned me once after the
marriage broke up. I don't know how she found out where I
lived—I was keeping such a low profile. She called me a
puttana, a whore, and said she wished she could kill me for
what I'd done to her family.''

It seemed tactless to mention she'd told me that already.

"What you'd done? Just having an affair?"

She inhaled audibly, straightening her spine. "No. But
that would have been enough. My husband broke my arm
when he found out.''

I must have looked shocked. She reached out as if to show
me the arm was okay now.

"The whole thing scared me. I mean, the way I'd been
raised, it was more emotion than I'd ever seen. I freaked.''

"You moved in with Edward."

"After Santina's phone call." She tilted her head. "I usually never talk about this. But I told you already, didn't I?
That someone broke into his apartment and raped me?"

"Not that part." My throat knotted. "Was this back in
seventy-one?''

Her turn to look surprised. She nodded. "Edward moved

out here a while later. I had family, an uncle, here and I came, too. We weren't in love or anything. He was in love with someone else. I couldn't handle a relationship of any kind. But we kept in touch for a while. Eventually I met Phil.''

I couldn't bring myself to ask, Did the rapist give you herpes? Did you pass it on to Edward?

A cloud covered the sun, making the sky dark. Objects in the periphery of my vision vanished. My attention was on Rita Delacort and nothing else. Pale freckled skin, intelligent eyes that corralled old hurts, a face projecting battle-scarred wariness.

Edward had asked me to do this woman a favor. A woman he'd lived with while I pined for him in jail.

I was conscious of wanting to feel something, of wondering what the appropriate feeling might be. I'd done anger often and intensely. It didn't feel right anymore.

''It was ironic, in a way.'' Elbows on her knees, she leaned closer to me. ''Here I was auditing Italian classes, reading all these Italian magazines that were obsessed with kidnapping—how to avoid kidnapping. That kidnappers don't snatch you in the morning when you're alert and on your way to work. That they wait till you're coming home after work, all spaced out and tired. And you know, that's just what happened. I was putting the key into Edward's door—he was emptying bedpans at a hospital, saving money to go to San Francisco—and wham, someone comes up behind me and pushes me in.''

I hoped she'd spare me the details. ''You got your first dog after that.''

''My uncle helped me get him. Really a police friend of my uncle's. Through the police department here.''

She collapsed back into the cushions of her redwood loveseat. "I don't usually talk about this. Really. I hope I'm not disgusting you."

I considered the previous year's conversations: about clothes, cars, court dockets and motions, loan agreements and writs of attachment, computerized sprinkler systems, vacations in Cabo. It almost hurt to talk about something real.

I changed the subject, returning to my agenda. "Your husband had a case before the judge I clerk for. I didn't know that when I talked to him. I didn't know until he went to the judge and asked him to disqualify himself. He said my going to see him implied some kind of judicial bias. So the case got reassigned—to a judge who'll be a lot more sympathetic to your husband's client."

Her brows pinched. She hadn't darkened them with pencil today; they were incongruously light beneath her mop of black curls.

"And I got into trouble," I added, though the trouble was mostly of my own making.

I waited—in vain—for a reply. I could see her throat ripple as if it were hard for her to speak. But maybe she was still thinking about the man in Edward's apartment. The thought surfaced: if I'd stayed in Boston a few months longer, it could have been me.

I said quickly, "When I talked to your husband, I thought he had an ace up his sleeve, that he might be contemplating some subtle form of revenge. Remember? Remember me saying that?"

A whispered "Yes."

"Do you think"—I focused on now, right now—"his revenge is that Edward works for him?"

Her skin went suddenly red, cheeks looking almost scalded. That's all; no other reaction.

"It makes sense, doesn't it?" I appealed to her. "Your husband hires Edward to tell him everything you're up to.

And also to help him manipulate a lawsuit to benefit an important client.''

''You say it makes sense.'' She made an impatient, chopping gesture. ''How often do things make sense?''

She had me there. ''Let me ask you, did you call your husband and tell him I was coming to visit him?''

She moistened her lips. ''Did I? I guess.''

''Because he was expecting me. If you didn't call him—''

''Maybe I did.''

''—then Edward called him. To let him know the job was done, that the judge's clerk was on her way.''

''What's the point of this?'' Rita's question was softly spoken, almost uninflected. ''This judge of yours, was he angry?''

''Not really. But it's certainly bad news for the plaintiffs in your husband's case. They're represented by Harry Prough.''

''Harry Prough,'' she repeated. ''Oh, no.''

''Your husband hires your ex-lover''—damn him, did he have to sleep with her while I was in jail?—''to spy on you. I run into him and he sees a way to really help your husband out—help him with a big case. Doesn't it make sense?''

She clasped her hands in her lap, looking infinitely weary. ''It would only make sense if I didn't trust Edward,'' she said.

My point exactly. The bastard. ''Look how well things turned out for your husband. And it's all Edward's doing— he sent me over here. Why should you trust him?''

''Why shouldn't I trust him? Because things turned out well for Phil?'' Bitterly, ''Things always turn out well for Phil. He wins his motions, he gets richer and richer, we all end up where he wants us. It has nothing to do with''—she shook her head, apparently groping for the right word—''with anything we can control. I couldn't hurt him and Edward couldn't help him, even if we wanted to.''

"What are we talking about?" I'd really had it with the kismet theory.

"Control," Rita Delacort said quietly. "We have no control, only choices."

She spoke quietly, but she might as well have used a bull-horn.

"Like my mother-in-law used to say." She pressed her fingers against her sinuses. "You cry for your sins and you pay your debts."

"Other people's debts."

"If other people are your sins."

23

THERE ARE THINGS I've done so often they should be automatic and stress-free; things I've done, at times, almost by rote. But just when I think I'm firmly in the groove, a change in perspective makes my routine suddenly repugnant.

It happened in the early seventies. After a half-dozen years of listening to vociferous radicals prove each other's views passé, I lost my tolerance for political meetings. The Weather Underground was ripping the heads off its leaders for not embracing (and later *for* embracing) Marxism, Aquarians were high on drugs and corny slogans, the Yippies were doing a cross between guerrilla theater and romper room, the Black Panthers were pretending to be Viet Cong, the SDS was scraping its scattered entrails off meeting-room floors, the Old Left was still fighting about Stalin and Castro and staging cozy vigils. I didn't think drugs or love—or even revolution for the hell of it—could take the place of boring old consensus-building. But I could no longer bear the strategizing and restrategizing, the infighting, the ideologues, the rhetoric and party lines. If that's what passed for consensus, what was the point? If we couldn't agree among ourselves, how could we ever persuade anyone else?

I remember trying to explain this to my parents. I remember telling them I'd overdosed on meetings. I remember raving about Trotskyites and Marxists and people who thought Marcuse had said it all in 1959, about the Woodstock nation and the Symbionese Liberation Army; and sure it was hard to admit we weren't stopping the war and building utopia, but was it really better to go round and round the hamster wheel? If we weren't accomplishing anything, why bother merely doing something?

Throughout my manic diatribe, my parents watched me with bland concern, occasionally whispering to each other on their sling-back couch. Then my father fixed me with his sad blue eyes and said that maybe I ought to break with the Old Left–influenced part of the New Left for a while (my parents were into lefty roots at the time, which made them a little unhip but very "grounded"). Perhaps a brief fling with the Yippies would do me good. Ever indulgent, they were basically suggesting an ideological vacation—suggesting I forget history for a while and throw some cream pies.

I kept on going to meetings, however frazzling and infuriating, for the next few years. As long as the war raged, I couldn't smoke pot in snug isolation, no matter what Timothy Leary preached. But my shift in attitude made me equate meetings with Turkish prisons. Today, you couldn't get me to a meeting at gunpoint.

Unfortunately, I am starting to feel that way about lawyer cocktail parties. For years, I've accepted them as part of my career, like law library dust and cranky judges. When I worked for Julian Warneke, it was Teamsters luncheons (complete with dancing girls in feathers and pasties), office open houses (ours and other firms') and weekly "working lunches." When I worked for Wailes, Roth, Fotheringham & Beck, it was endless client parties, associate "retreats," wine-tastings for the summer clerks, judges'-night dinners. Lawyer parties, especially big-firm parties, are a little less fun than standing in a closet full of blue suits. You paste on a smile (the more smug and superior, the better you'll fit in) and discuss one of the four things lawyers talk about: work, workouts, foreign cars, domestic wines. If you don't have a workout routine or know much about wine, you nod a lot.

I'd been doing it for years; I had my smiling and nodding down pat. So why all of a sudden did it seem like unprecedented torture, standing in a room full of lawyers, the usual catered plastic goblet in my hand? Why did my smile suddenly come unstuck? I was standing in Judge Shanna's chambers wondering if being bored to death by lawyers was really better than being harangued by Trotskyites. A three-day weekend of serious substance abuse had not made me more charitable.

George McLeod was standing beside me looking as ill at ease as I felt. "The other judges have Christmas parties for their clerks and former clerks—clerks, that's all. Judge Shanna's the only one who has a day-after-Labor Day party for everyone in the world."

George was not exaggerating, not much anyway. Every attorney who had ever appeared before or was ever likely to appear before the judge found it politic to be present. Several other judges had come—but not Rondi, thank God. As a result, the judge's chambers, the outer office, the clerks' office, even the corridors outside were packed with standing suits.

The judge's chambers were full of jovial men drinking, mingling, laughing. They were relentlessly amiable, in fact—compensating for being assholes in their pleadings? The handful of women in the room looked a little stiff, and their smiles seemed a little forced. There was a men's-club aura about Shanna's chambers even when they weren't crowded with men postmorteming racquetball games.

One of the men was Philip Delacort. He was standing with two lawyers from White, Sayres & Speck, an aristocratic firm whose associates drive cars resembling small spacecraft. The men were doing some us-guys guffawing and armpunching when Delacort glanced over and spotted me. He said something to his companions and began maneuvering through the crowd toward me, murmuring into the hair of a woman or two along the way.

I'd have liked to have insinuated myself into a group, any group. George had been drawn off by one of the judge's former clerks. There was a nerdy couple on my right discussing a probate hearing, and two women on my left wondered whether one au pair was enough for two children. As desperately as I wanted to clique into their conversations, I had literally nothing to say on either subject.

When Delacort approached, I had no choice but to speak to him.

He was grinning, somewhat tentatively. "I wanted to say hello. Tell you I hope I didn't bring anything down on your head." He shrugged. "Just doing what I needed to do for my client."

In my long years of socializing with lawyers, how many times had I heard some variation of this? Sorry I had to call you an incompetent Nazi in my pleadings, buddy; just trying to make my client look good. Sorry I threatened to sue you personally, pal; just trying to get you to back off on the motion to compel.

The required response was, Don't worry about it; it's all in the game. But I'm not as good at the game as I used to be.

I said, "I assume Edward Hershey works for you."

"Edward Hershey, as far as I know, used to be a good friend, quote unquote, of my wife's." Delacort had the kind of open, blue-eyed face that radiated honesty—no wonder he was a trial lawyer. "I gather he's the 'mutual friend' who sent you to see me?"

I nodded. My neck and shoulders were starting to compress like a spring. "You knew that. You were expecting me—Edward must have called you."

"Rita left a message on my machine. But I suspected Hershey set it up. Rita tends to turn to others—or else let the problem overwhelm her." He smiled slightly, as if at some private joke. "Luckily she has me."

We were only six inches apart in the crowded room. Above the murmur of probate lawyers and au pair–deficient mothers, the judge could be heard to boom, "What a candidate he was! Cutting through the formality!" Good old "Call me Jimmy" Carter.

"Just so we're clear between us," Delacort continued, "I didn't arrange our meeting in any way." He regarded me with an arch squint of the eye. "You didn't either, now did you?"

I was too appalled to speak. Why would I seek out a lawyer whose case was pending before my judge? I'd have to be a fool. Or a secretly interested party.

George appeared suddenly, wedging himself in beside Delacort. "I was working on your securities fraud case before it got reassigned," he butted in.

Delacort was apparently unwilling to broaden the discussion to include another person. He looked over my right shoulder, saying, "Do I see Chardonnay on the sideboard?"

"I'm sure you do." There were lawyers present, weren't there?

"Get you a glass?" he offered.

"No, thanks." Not if it meant having to talk to him again.

As Delacort pushed by me, I noticed Judge Shanna, half an auburn head shorter than any other man in the room, watching us.

I suggested to George that we go make sure no one was having sex on our desktops. He looked so shocked I almost regretted saying it.

We pushed through chambers and through the reception room, where the crowd seemed more ill at ease and less well dressed. We slid into our office, past two women discussing the "X factor," an apparently undefined quality their firm felt they lacked.

One of them lamented, "Steve bills fewer hours than we do and he's a complete jellyfish with clients. And they don't have any problem with *his* X."

To which the other woman replied, "Men have a presumption of X."

Don't they just.

Also in the small room were three men pulling federal reporters off the shelves. Two of them were young and slightly rumpled. (I was beginning to detect a pattern: the farther from chambers, the less natty one was required to be.) The third was Harry Prough, his gray Jewish Afro mashed in parts, sticking out in others, as if he'd slept on it and forgotten to comb it.

Prough was saying, "How can you have any respect for precedent?" Whereupon he opened a supreme court reporter and began reading from the racist Dred Scott decision.

Midway through a paragraph about why blacks could not be citizens despite Congress's insistent efforts, he glanced up and noticed me. With no regard for his rapt audience, he slammed the book closed and approached me.

"Willa Jansson," he said.

I was flattered that he remembered me. I'd seen him more than once at rallies, meetings, luncheons, but I'd only had one real conversation with him.

"Clement Kerrey was just talking to me about you."

Despite obvious dissimilarities—the back-off frown, the snidely pinched lips—Prough reminded me of Clement. Maybe it was just the politics. It could easily have been Warneke, Prough instead of Warneke, Kerrey.

Prough squinted as if trying to divine my thoughts. If he was looking for assurances of my political correctness, he would be disappointed.

"I need another person in my office." He dropped the law book on my desk and began patting the pockets of his skimpy, too-light suit. "Call me when you're done clerking." From his breast pocket he extracted a business card.

I took the card with a mumbled "Thank you." And was conscious of an internal voice saying, No way—I hate being a lawyer.

Why did I have to have a midlife crisis now, with the prospect of an interesting job before me? Why not last year, when I was offered an upscale version of the life of Ivan Denisovich?

"Clement's recommendation is good enough for me," Prough continued.

Bless all the old radicals like Clement, trying to get their red-diaper babies established in the world.

I looked at Harry Prough's pinched, unpleasant face and saw a collage of old lefties, lefties of my parents' generation. Maybe they were ideologically procrustean, long-winded, simplistically dismissive of other points of view. But they were kind. To me, they had always been kind.

"I used to sit in on your trials," I told Prough. "I was always impressed—"

He waved away my praise. "It's an act you perfect with practice."

"You're not a true believer?"

"True believer!" He all but snorted. "Sure, I'm a believer—in the power of persuasion. The theater of ideas. Your clients"—again he waved his hand—"they could be anybody. You don't want to be in a position of screening clients for moral rectitude. If you want to believe in an idea then certainly the First Amendment, the Fourth Amendment. But the only real commandment is that prison sucks and you keep anybody out of there that you can."

I nodded. Prison does suck.

From just behind me, George chimed in, "Doesn't it trouble you what a tremendous waste of resources it is, trying cases that except for a technicality would have been plea-bargained?"

Prough blinked a few times. "No."

"You represent the plaintiff class in—"

"I know you," Prough interrupted. "You're the other clerk. You dicked around with that case."

"If we're talking about—"

"I've only got one class action. What in the hell happened to that case? Why did Shanna disqualify himself?"

Prough squinted at George, leaning forward to allow the X-factor women to thread behind him and leave the office. Prough's young acolytes fiddled nervously with the law books, talking quietly.

George glanced at me with obvious hesitation.

Oh, fuck. "There's a woman called Rita Delacort," I began. "Philip Delacort's wife."

"Yeah, so?"

"I was asked by a friend"—God, what was I saying?—"a

friend of *hers*, to talk to Delacort. About family issues surrounding their divorce.''

His face shut down. His eyes were like a dark room.

Beside me, George cleared his throat. Was it a breach of ethics for me to talk about this?

''I didn't know Delacort had a case before Judge—''

Prough interrupted. ''That's it?''

''That's it.''

''You didn't discuss the securities case with Delacort?''

''No.''

''You talked to Delacort about his wife, and for that the judge disqualified himself?''

''Yes.''

Prough shook his head slowly. ''I've been practicing before the federal bench for a total of twenty-four years. I've been appearing before Shanna since the day he began hearing cases.'' More head-shaking. ''And you know what, I don't buy it. It doesn't ring true.''

I could feel George breathing on my hair. The young men at the bookshelf were quiet now, watching Prough.

''Delacort complained,'' I said. ''The judge only had the case three weeks. He thought it might drag on for years—he didn't want to risk a several-year case getting thrown out on appeal.''

Prough rolled his eyes. ''Come on, listen to what you're saying. Mike Shanna worried about getting overturned on appeal?''

A couple of the judge's former clerks charged through the doorway, saying, ''Talk about bringing back memories! Even the way it smells!''

They were followed by the judge himself, large in presence if not stature.

''Harry!'' he boomed, clapping Prough on the back.

Prough grinned and nodded. "Judge," he said, with significantly less bonhomie.

"You've met my new clerk?"

Prough glanced at me. "Got her father out of jail once, Judge. Fortunately, he was just passing through."

Prough represented my father? I supposed most lefty lawyers had, at one time or another.

Prough continued, "He was in there long enough to get the crap kicked out of him by a guard we used to call Attila. Federal prison, by the way."

I backed into George. My father never told me about Attila.

Prough looked suddenly weary. "It's a fact of life in there."

I tried not to visualize it. The cheerful man who made me Szechwan tofu and grew greens for me in his garden. How could he put himself in that position? How could he risk savage beatings for nothing, for symbols?

"A good man," Prough concluded. Then more cynically, "Idealists usually do end up at the wrong end of the boot, eh, Judge?"

Judge Shanna's lips were slightly pursed, his gray eyes glazed and cold. He smiled weakly and turned to his former clerks, who were standing at the window pointing out familiar landmarks—remembering them patched with plywood and hung with yellow tags. "Glad you could make it, Harry," he said, stepping past us.

Harry Prough watched him with a malicious half-smile.

Then he turned to me. His head jerked backward and his brows lifted. "Hey, maybe it's not your dad I'm thinking of."

My father had never told me about Attila. About any of the Attilas he'd encountered.

I'd tried to take care of him; keep him safe. For my sake,

because it hurt to the point of nausea imagining him at the wrong end of a boot.

The judge laughed with his former clerks, drawing George into the group.

I made myself focus on their conversation, about what had happened to the Federal Building during the earthquake: bookcases and file cabinets emptying, a four-foot pile of papers and books to be reshelved.

"It took us days," one clerk said.

"Cheaper than hiring janitors," said the other.

I curled Harry Prough's card into my fist, watching him watch the foursome. Prough hadn't mentioned the securities case to the judge. Why should he? Once the judge decided to disqualify himself, complaining became useless. Judges were expected to err on the side of caution, after all.

Prough stared at the judge, the hint of a noncommittal smile on his lips.

Err on the side of caution. Since when did Judge Shanna err on the side of caution? Since when did he worry about being overruled on appeal?

Harry Prough was right. It didn't ring true.

Prough turned to me, his smile broadening. "Sneak downstairs with me for five minutes."

I was flattered. As many lefty lawyers as I'd met, Harry Prough still impressed me. Maybe because he was one of the few I hadn't gotten to know. I pushed the thought of Julian Warneke back under the ice.

We ambled down to the sixteenth floor, to the Federal Building's generic cafeteria—beige, overlighted, haunted by overcooked beans, burnt coffee and stale tobacco. We staked out a back table and played it safe with bottled juice.

Harry Prough cocked his head. "Wailes, Roth—is that what Clement told me? What was that about?"

Et tu, Harry? "It was about money."

"Money." He pursed his lips and shook his head.

"They made me a job offer when I needed a job." I let it go at that. I didn't mention being appalled by the offer until I learned the job carried a salary of ninety thousand.

"Wish I'd known. You could have come to me then."

I noticed Harry wore the oblivious, haggard look I associated with my former employers; the look of someone who'd stopped questioning and thrown himself into the grand maw.

"I was a little soured at the time," I admitted.

"Soured about . . . ?"

Part of me counseled caution, reminded me he was a potential employer. Another part of me wanted it out there, no surprises. Wanted to avoid a rerun of my two years with Julian Warneke.

"I had some problems with Julian's firm. The five-hundred-dollar working lunches with just the right wines—that's what you'd expect from Wailes, Roth, maybe. But in an antielitist, for-the-little-guy firm . . ." I slid my elbows forward on the tabletop. "And cases becoming political props, excuses to climb on a soapbox—"

"Gotcha." Prough nodded impatiently. "My trip is keep the client out of jail, end of story. Maybe sometimes you gain a larger freedom by sacrificing someone's liberty. But my bottom line is, it won't be my client's liberty. Not if I can help it."

Exactly what I wanted to hear.

"I miss the clients," I admitted. "I miss working for people instead of banks and corporations." And judges. "Even the maddening parts." Trying to make them understand that it didn't matter what was fair; only what was legal, what was arguable.

"Don't get me wrong." Prough was staring into the distance. "I think Warneke was a hell of an admirable guy."

I felt myself stiffen. I didn't want to talk about Julian. The firm, okay; not the man.

"You really have to give him credit." Prough took a quick swallow of juice. "He could take a piddly-ass little case and turn it into Armageddon, Right versus Left. And you know, I think in some ways he was absolutely correct. Those cases were Armageddon."

"Meaning the Left got apocalypsed."

"Yeah. Still is."

I found the sentiment refreshing. The world is filled with sixties Pollyannas who believe the "best" of the decade got mainstreamed, and that the rest somehow doesn't matter.

"My view, we got mowed down and they sowed the ground with salt. We're left diddlyfucking around with no organization, no numbers, no will. They find a cure for AIDS, children of eighties' yuppies will get sexual and maybe antimaterialistic again, and then maybe politics will swing back. In the meantime, it's keep as many lefties out of jail as we can. I hate to harp on it, but I think it's that simple."

I could almost hear my father scoff that of course it wasn't that simple. That cynicism, not political reality, is that simple.

I didn't reply.

"That's what it comes down to for me. For my practice." His eyes glittered as he watched me. "That's what I want in an associate. Somebody practical enough to pursue an end, not an agenda, you know what I mean?"

I must have embraced that goal a hundred times in arguments with my parents. And I'd certainly resented the inverse in Julian's firm. But, smiling my assent at Harry Prough, I was suddenly uncomfortable with his "practicality." I felt like I was looking into a political mirror and seeing a vampiric blank.

24

"GEORGE," I SAID, "tell me again about the securities fraud case."

He looked pale and puffy-eyed, wiping the last drops of spilled Perrier off his desk. "You want the files?"

"Yes." I dropped some party napkins into the trash. The judge's former clerk was right—we were cheaper than janitors.

"They got sent over to Rondi's office. Since he's keeping the case."

"What about your work product?" Our task was to analyze documents and write bench memos for the judge, telling him what the law was and how it governed the situation before him. The bench memos were considered "work product"—confidential correspondence from clerk to judge—and they would forever remain in this office.

"I don't know." He yawned, looking out the huge windows at the glow of an anemic sunset. "I was looking for that stuff—it's not in here anymore. Judge Shanna must have it. Ask Margaret tomorrow."

"George," I said again.

"What?" He continued looking out the window, absently rebuttoning his top shirt button.

"Tell me about the case."

He tightened the knot of his tie. "Junk bonds. We went through this."

"You said junk bonds are basically—"

"I don't suppose you'd like to have dinner with me and my father?"

I looked across our back-to-back, littered desks. George still stared morosely at the pale yellow sky. For a second, I thought I'd hallucinated the invitation.

Then he looked at me, repeating, "Want to have dinner with me and my father?"

"I didn't know your family lived around here," I hedged.

"They don't. My father lives in Manhattan. He's passing through on business." George looked mighty grim about it. "I've been summoned to dinner."

"I shouldn't butt in. He'll want some private time—"

"I don't!" George sat perfectly still, red-cheeked and in a sudden sweat.

Well, well. "You don't get along?"

He pinched his lips together so that he appeared to have a solid, unbroken beard from nose to collar. "We always have," he murmured. "Everyone says we could be clones." If so, he didn't look happy about it. "But I thought if you were free . . . ?"

It sounded like the kind of dinner where you sit and smile

until you sink into a social coma. But I knew begging when I heard it.

"Sure, I guess so." Why rush home to sit by myself?

The stiffness went out of George's posture. "Good. That's good. He should be here pretty soon."

The prediction was fulfilled five minutes later, when the intercom on Margaret's desk buzzed. George motioned me to follow him to the outer office. Wanting me with him when his father pushed through the door?

A moment later, a florid, well-dressed man stepped into the room. The first thing he said was, "What's that?"

George flinched, reflexively touching his beard.

Maybe George would look a little like his father if he gained sixty pounds, but I didn't think he was in much danger of being mistaken for a clone otherwise.

As George introduced me, his father's gaze kept wandering to the beard.

"George mentioned that you're here on business?" I'll say this about meeting other people's parents—it makes me appreciate mine. (But why did Mother set up that "accidental" meeting between me and Hershey? Could she really be matchmaking? At my age?)

George's father forced himself to stop staring at the beard. He smiled at me, shaking my hand. "I work for a brokerage firm—one of the largest and oldest, as a matter of fact—and I do travel fairly often ancillary to my transactions. But this particular trip is politics, not business."

George was standing beside his father now, his shoulders high and his arms locked across his chest. "Republican National Committee."

"Oh." I smiled, beginning the slow descent into social narcosis.

But however long dinner seemed to me, I suspect it seemed much longer to George.

The only thing that redeemed it from my point of view was George's father's explanation of junk bonds, which he concluded with the lament, ''We still consider them quite a glamorous innovation, to tell the truth, and we're gung ho about them—or we were before various corporations started getting sued for fraud.'' He pushed away the dessert he had previously attacked with gusto. ''Fraud! What a load of malarkey. I don't see how a buyer can buy a bond—clearly identified as such—and then expect it to turn into stock when it's time to go trade it. We feel like the vultures are circling—vestiges of antienterprise attitudes we thought had died out in the seventies.''

George set his coffee cup down with a clank, apparently steeling himself for an onslaught.

And sure enough, his father added, ''And what does my own son do but go to work for the most crazy-eyed radical on the federal bench!''

25

JUDGE RONDI'S COURTROOM was an exact duplicate of Judge Shanna's—gray carpet, oak rail and pews, tastefully upholstered jurors' chairs, marble wall with kiddie-pool-sized United States and California seals behind the judge's bench. More expensive and more dignified than state-court decor; therefore more intimidating to some, more comforting to others. Spectators were usually more subdued here, corporate clients more relaxed. Certainly the three men at the table with Philip Delacort appeared unworried. Harry Prough's small investors, had they shown up, might have been awed by the cold bureaucratic grandeur.

I sat in the back pew. I could almost hear Julian Warneke's eloquent diatribe about the word "fuck"—part of the oath I'd flung at a Presidio M.P. Julian had revved proudly into my defense, and I'd listened and found it stirring—for a while. Then I'd begun to notice Rondi reddening and fidgeting and clenching his fists, until it seemed to me he was about to detonate. I'd suddenly realized that hiring Julian meant staging a show instead of mounting a defense. It had been a good show—much applause from the pews—but it had had nothing to do with winning acquittal. I'd watched Julian and I'd felt helpless, doomed, thrown away. I'd watched the federal marshal absentmindedly buff his handcuffs.

We have no control, only choices; that's what Rita Delacort had said. I'd chosen Julian to be my lawyer. Later, I'd chosen him to be my employer.

I remembered his funeral. A Teamster client had played the organ: "Which Side Are You On, Boys."

Now, the bailiff announced that this court was in session, the Honorable Manolo M. Rondi presiding. I watched Rondi billow in.

He cleared his throat and said, "Gentlemen, I have read your papers and am prepared to proceed. Mr. Delacort, this is your motion. If you would like to say something before I rule, please do so."

"Your Honor," Delacort stood health-club straight, exuding confidence, "you know from our moving papers that there is no material issue of fact here; that the facts are largely undisputed and that my client is entitled to judgment as a matter of law. My client discharged its duty to disclose by offering the plaintiffs access to the public financial records of the companies in question before the sale of the bonds and—"

"Yes, yes, Mr. Delacort," Rondi interrupted. "I've read your papers, I know all that. Please limit your remarks to that which I do not already know."

Delacort hesitated. But he knew Rondi, knew Rondi's stand on white-collar crime. He could afford to let this one slide. "Well, Your Honor, I think we set out our argument rather thoroughly in our papers."

"That you did, Mr. Delacort." He motioned him to be seated. "Mr. Prough? Do you have anything to add to your papers?"

Harry Prough stood slowly.

He said, "Sixteen investors, Your Honor, have sworn in their complaints that no one—not one employee of the defendant corporation—ever explained to them what 'junk bonds' are, ever even used that term to describe the investment they were asked to make. Sixteen investors, Your Honor, were not told that these bonds, unlike bonds issued by blue-chip corporations, represented a debt load capable of sinking the bond-issuing corporation"—he snapped his fingers—"just like that. Sixteen investors were not told that it is virtually impossible to trade junk bonds on the open market. So when Mr. Delacort stands there and says that the facts are largely undisputed, I agree. But when he says his client fulfilled its duty to disclose—"

"Stop!" Rondi held up a shaking hand. "This is all in your papers, Mr. Prough."

"Your Honor—"

"Don't finish the sentence, Mr. Prough, unless it is information I do not already have before me!"

Prough's hands curled. "Your Honor, my sense is that you intend to rule against my clients."

"That's absolutely correct, Mr. Prough."

Prough pulled a sheaf of fanfold computer paper out of his briefcase. "Since nineteen fifty-nine, Your Honor, you have ruled against investor-plaintiffs in securities fraud cases every single time such cases have come before you. A total of twenty-one times, Your Honor, eighteen of them on summary judgment motions, so that plaintiffs were not even allowed their day in court."

Rondi's jaw dropped. He stiffened, as if recovering from a blow.

"Furthermore, Your Honor, you chose to hear this case when it was submitted to you for reassignment in your role as temporary presiding judge. You could have assigned the case to any of nineteen other judges, but you kept it. Given the statistics on prior securities cases before you, Your Honor . . ." He stopped, his shoulders climbing, his stance tensing into fight-or-flight.

I couldn't believe it, couldn't believe Prough's guts. I wanted to stand and applaud.

"What—*what* are you accusing me of, Mr. Prough?" Rondi stood halfway out of his chair. He seemed ready to leap off the bench and tackle Prough.

Beside me, George whispered, "Holy shit."

Prough stepped out from behind the table. "As you know, federal court cases are randomly assigned by computer. There's a possibility of subverting this randomness, Your Honor, when a case goes before a presiding judge for reassignment. If the presiding judge takes into account the type of action in question, and decides to seize the opportunity to hold onto the case and express his personal—"

"Are you accusing me—" Rondi leaned heavily on his robed arms, his wizened head trembling. "If you are impugning my partiality, Mr. Prough"—he sneered the name—"you would be well advised to raise the issue before the judicial performance committee rather than creating a spectacle in my courtroom! Mr. Prough!"

"My preference at this time, Your Honor, is to move pursuant to Title Twenty-eight, section one forty-four, that, in light of this statistical material, you disqualify yourself from hearing this motion and order reassignment of the case."

I punched George's shoulder, much to his surprise, and smiled at him.

"You are coming dangerously close to being in contempt of this court, Mr. Prough." The old fascist's eyes glittered. "You know very well how to file such a motion—if such was ever your intention—and you know very well— But enough! No more! I will now proceed to render my ruling on the summary judgment motion appropriately before me."

"Your Honor," Prough persisted, "I move that you disqualify yourself and submit this case to the next judge in line for reassignment."

"I said *enough*, Mr. Prough! At this time I will enter my—"

"I'm afraid I will have to insist that you disqualify yourself and—"

"You have gone too far!" The words came out in a strangled fury. "Too far! You are in contempt of court!" He gestured to the federal marshals. "Defendant's summary judgment motion is granted, and you, Mr. Prough, will be held in custody until such time as you are willing to come before this court and withdraw your spurious innuendoes and make appropriate apologies to the bench!"

"I will not withdraw a meritorious motion, Your Honor."

"There is no such motion before me, Mr. Prough, because you have not properly submitted one!"

Prough held up a large red paperback—*Federal Civil Judicial Procedure and Rules*. "Sections One forty-four and Four fifty-five entitle me to demand your disqualification in light of clear evidence of a pro-white-collar-defendant prejudice in your previous rulings."

The federal marshals hung back until Rondi gestured to them with renewed vigor.

Delacort, watching the marshals approach Prough, looked like a billboard model, no facial expression, posture perfect.

I watched the marshals handcuff Harry Prough, conscious of the stir among the handful of other spectators. One of them, whom I recognized as the legal reporter for the afternoon paper, dashed out of the courtroom.

"Free Harry Prough," I heard myself mutter. If only I had a placard.

I watched the marshals march Prough across the courtroom and out the side door. I knew where they were taking him: to the prisoners' elevator for a quick ride up to the jail.

I hoped Prough reacted to the place with greater dignity than I had. I hoped he didn't slide down the cold wall and spend most of the night crying. But then, he wasn't looking at two months.

Or maybe he was. He'd already said he wouldn't withdraw his motion.

I imagined myself locked up until I promised to eat Rondi's shit. How long would it take me to capitulate?

I wondered what I could do for Prough. I might be working for him soon, if he was serious about having me; I should do something for him now. I could help him file an appeal, if he'd let me.

Judge Rondi looked clamp-jawed and pale, staring at the door through which the marshals had led Prough. Then his gaze drifted to the back of the courtroom.

For a charged moment, he looked at me, eyes narrowing. Two months in jail because the old bastard didn't like "young ladies" to use the word "fuck." But Harry Prough would get him this time. Every day Harry Prough spent in jail, local media would be examining his charge that Rondi was prejudiced in favor of white-collar criminals. The more clever reporters might notice that Rondi was also prejudiced against political activists and minority defendants. The resulting splash could discredit Rondi right into early retirement.

I smiled at the old Nazi to let him know I'd enjoy every minute of his public embarrassment.

And for a second there, he looked as though he was going to send the marshals after me.

26

"I SN'T HARRY PROUGH great?" I gushed again to George.

George shrugged. He'd removed his suit jacket and loosened his tie in belated acknowledgment that Margaret and Judge Shanna had gone home an hour ago.

"You're so results oriented." That was George's idea of a scathing insult.

He pushed a copy of *Federal Procedure* toward me. "Remember the code sections Prough quoted? Take a look."

George had them bookmarked. I skimmed the first section, subtitled "Bias or prejudice of judge." Skimmed it, then read it more carefully. Then closed the book, feeling terrible.

"See what I mean?" George needled me. "Prough was supposed to file an affidavit *before* the proceeding. If he'd filed an affidavit saying Rondi was prejudiced, the matter would have gone automatically to another judge. Automatically.''

He reached over, pulling the book back and reading, '' 'Whenever a party to any proceeding in a district court makes and files a timely and sufficient affidavit that the judge before whom the matter is pending has a personal bias or prejudice either against him or in favor of any adverse party, such judge shall proceed no further therein, but another judge shall be assigned to hear such proceeding.' ''

''I get the point, George.'' Either Harry Prough hadn't really cared about disqualifying Rondi or he hadn't believed he could prove prejudice. He'd been putting on a show, goading Rondi, maybe even hoping to be cited for contempt.

Harry Prough had been carrying on the tradition of Julian Warneke, in fact. In spite of all he'd said to me yesterday, he'd staged a show. And I'd sat there admiring in Harry what I'd so disdained in Julian—the decision to make a statement instead of win a case.

''The other section's troubling, too.'' He scratched his beard. ''For different reasons. But the point is, you're results oriented. You don't like Rondi, so you don't care how he's challenged—legitimately or illegitimately.''

That part was true.

''Well,'' George closed his *Federal Procedure*, ''I suppose it makes sense from a results standpoint. An affidavit would have gotten Rondi off the case, but it wouldn't have put Rondi on trial with the press.''

Also true. But my feelings about it were no longer unmixed.

''You know Judge Shanna interceded with Rondi this afternoon? To release Prough?'' To George's credit, he sounded proud of Shanna.

"Yes." Several other judges had done the same, probably hoping to avert a flurry of sensationalistic news stories.

But as much as I wanted Harry Prough out of jail, I was glad for once that Rondi was a stubborn old cuss. Prough had, as George observed, put Rondi on trial. Let the press do to Rondi what he'd been doing to others since 1959.

And yet . . . Prough had staged an event instead of filing an affidavit. It troubled me that he'd done so in apparent contradiction to his courtroom philosophy. It troubled me even more that the result seemed so damned worthy—so damned worth it—when it wasn't my freedom on the line.

My politics seemed to depend on my personal convenience. I might as well be a Republican.

27

CLEMENT KERREY CLASPED both my hands, kissed my cheeks, smiled his crooked-toothed smile. With characteristic and reassuring corniness, he said of course it was okay, my dropping by without calling first, that I was family.

I looked around his Eureka Valley house, a small two-story rowhouse with a bit of deck and a small, weedy yard. It was in one of San Francisco's warmer neighborhoods—a sheltered mini-suburbia interspersed with the usual tacquerias, Chinese groceries and gay bars. It suited Clement, who even on this chilly evening wore sandals and short-sleeved cambric.

The interior was stacked with books and files. The furniture reminded me of my parents'—Cost Plus hodgepodge. But it was merely a backdrop for rows and rows of framed photographs of working people. Some were duplicates of those he'd given my parents. Others were more interesting, varied to include strippers, policemen, ball players—not just politically correct and unionized labor.

I sat in a hanging basket chair and Clement took a fan-back rattan.

"How nice!" Clement repeated. "How nice to see you."

"I was thinking about you. I heard your name yesterday. From Harry Prough."

"What a rascal Harry is." Clement grinned, a bit of the old sparkle back in his eyes. "Quite a bit of talk about him today."

"He could have filed an affidavit, Clement. He didn't have to dare Rondi to throw him in jail."

Clement's grin widened. "Ah, but Harry made his point. And you know, he's not afraid of a little jail time. Not after, what, four years he served?"

"Four years," I confirmed, my stomach knotting.

"A day or two—just long enough for the news stories, give him a shot at getting the case appealed—and then he apologizes. Not such a big deal." He began to look concerned, leaning closer and patting my hand.

"Thanks for talking to him about me, by the way."

He nodded, searching my face. "You were such an asset to us, to me and Julian. I keep thinking it's a shame you had to find another kind of work."

Talk about putting a good face on things. What I'd needed to find was another kind of salary.

"I think you and Harry would be good for each other. Accomplish some good stuff."

"Do you?" I could hear the edge in my voice; I wasn't even trying to keep the mask up. "After this last year, I don't know if I even want to try. I don't know how I feel about it."

With a law professor's exactness, he asked, "What's 'it'?"

"The sixties, the seventies, movement politics, the Left—whatever it was we were doing. I mean, I still think the Salvadorans should get sanctuary and the Nicaraguans should be left alone and the homeless should get federal money so they can keep warm. I still believe all that. I just"—a hard thing to say aloud—"I just don't want to be involved myself. I want someone else to get tired and angry and frustrated. I want someone else to deal with the stupid cranks and their secret agendas. Not me. I don't want to do it. And I don't want to feel obligated to do it."

I expected him to look shocked, to hit me with disapproval. Instead, he nodded. "That's why Julian and I started the firm, you know. Karma yoga—speaking through your work. My views were regarded as eccentric by many people on the Left"—a wry smile—"as you may recall. The Teamsters weren't popular in spite of being, in my opinion, one of the most together unions—the locals, I mean—that this or any country has ever seen. And all the grape boycott business . . ." He sighed. "They'd have chewed me up in meetings—the SDS, the Yippies, just about anybody. Not so much Julian—he was willing to let a few flowers bloom—maybe not a thousand, but a few. Anyway, I never felt obliged to go the meetings route. I preferred to do good in the workplace."

I supposed that was why, in his quasi-parental way, Clement had been talking me up to liberal judges and radical lawyers.

And I supposed that was the difference between us. Clement had considered his work politically correct and taken satisfaction from its social utility. I'd worked for Clement in the same legal and political environment, and all I'd done was see the ironies. I'd resented Julian for underpaying and overworking me in the name of the working-class struggle. I'd cast a critical eye on his partners—driving their turbo

Saabs, sipping their varietal wines, taking clients out on their sailboats.

"But then," he continued, "I come from a very work-ethic family. It's my basic assumption, that you speak through your work."

"Why did you stop? With your reputation, you could have started a new firm in a minute. Your labor clients would have stayed with you."

He closed his eyes tightly, his forehead and cheeks clenching into deep wrinkles. "Not without Julian. I couldn't do it without Julian."

And yet, Julian hadn't handled any labor matters—hadn't done much of anything except be a high-visibility figurehead.

"Why?" Tell me what Julian meant to you so I can try to guess what he meant to me. So I'll know why I can't bear to think about him, much less mourn him.

He opened his eyes, blinking rapidly as if to clear his vision. "I've thought about this a lot." He sounded a little apologetic. "Julian's strength as a lawyer and a political force was his ability to project himself as something larger and grander than himself—larger than one lawyer, I mean. He knew instinctively how to manipulate symbols." Another pause. "Are you all right?"

"His ability to manipulate symbols—his preference for doing that—it put a lot of people in jail, Clement—people who could have pleaded out easily." Be honest. Trust Clement, at least; that's why you came here. "People like me. Like my parents."

He looked a little wary. "But don't you think those clients made that choice to begin with?"

"We got swept up in a tide of romanticism about the revolution. We were young and stupid!"

He shook his head. "Not your parents. They're veterans from way back even before the Freedom Rider days."

"Where did that leave me? Did Julian ever think about me when he advised them to pour blood on draft files? Or made a big show of their trial?"

Clement sat up straighter in the rattan chair. "You stayed with Julian and Bess once, when you were a baby. Do you remember that?"

"No."

He shrugged. "We were always careful when children were involved. If the parents didn't have a support system, we did what we could. Sometimes the secretaries helped out."

I looked at Clement and thought, What's the point? What's the point of trying to convince a cerebral old bachelor that children aren't puppies, to be cared for by whoever happens to have drawn a suspended sentence; that a child's terror of separation, especially when accompanied by rough gun-toting men hauling the parents away, deserves more thought than maybe the secretaries can help out.

"Your parents," Clement said quietly, "look at the world with a deep sense of pain and guilt. They could no more sit back and do nothing than they could go out and torture po-litical prisoners personally. You of all people must realize the immediacy their ideals have for them."

Oh, yes, don't I ever. How many times had I seen Mother in a frenzy of anger over the treatment of some poor farmer or poor prisoner or poor immigrant?

"You might not feel that way, or feel that way with such intensity, Willa. But can you imagine having such a strong emotional reaction to injustice and doing *nothing?* You'd tear yourself apart."

"I had a strong emotional reaction to the Vietnam War."

He nodded vigorously. "And you were out on the streets marching. You knew about villagers being burned with na-palm and half a million soldiers dying. What could you do but react with your presence? What else would have seemed honest?''

"But it turned out to be so futile, Clement. We raised the cost of the war, and maybe that was a factor in getting us out of there—eventually. But in the process we discredited our best liberals and turned the New Left into something so desperate and crazy, so reactive that it withered away when the war ended.'' I knotted my fingers into my hair. "I don't think we'll ever reclaim power from the conservatives. I think Jimmy Carter blew our only chance."

Clement's shoulders drooped, his face relaxed. "This is causing you a lot of pain, isn't it?"

Stated baldly, it was an embarrassing proposition. Here I was, tormented by fifteen-year-old political angst. And I'd been thinking of *Clement* as cerebral. "I guess it does. You're right about me feeling like I had no choice—like I had to be on the streets protesting the war, just to live with myself. But I hated every minute of it. It made my life pure hell''—in jail especially—"and now I feel like it had no lasting effect. Democrats still run unpopular vice presidents and pander to the Right, radicals still tear each other up and hate each other for ideological impurity, liberals still let ideologues steamroll over them and shut them up.''

I felt myself blush. And why shouldn't I? Once again, I analyzed history according to my grumpy sense of having been personally inconvenienced.

"Do you resent people who participated because they enjoyed it?''

People like my parents. "Maybe I do. For acting like the rest of us should be doing more. Like we should still be doing something.''

"You don't think we should, Willa? With the kind of problems we're having in this country? With the kind of training you have? Your specialized ability to use your law degree to help people?''

I looked at him in his unassuming shirtsleeves and sandals, surrounded by striking black-and-white portraits of working people, and I was reminded again of the old organizing song—Julian's dirge: *Which side are you on, boys, which side are you on?*

''I guess I do think so, Clement, or why would I be talking to you?''

He looked a little startled.

''I should be doing something and I don't want to, I absolutely don't want to. Because it's a bore and a frustration and a terrible waste of my time and energy.''

''You feel you get that from your parents—that 'should' quality.''

''Yes. Maybe.'' I hugged myself. I felt bloodlessly cold, my skin rising in goosebumps. ''Not completely.''

''That brings me back to Julian.'' He sighed. ''We disagreed on so many issues. He took the lefter-than-thou position; I lined up behind the unions, wherever they were. I guess you could say he was newer Left than I was.'' Behind him, portraits showed workers' faces twisting with effort as they loaded boxes, flung off their garments, separated fighting men. ''But Julian's sense of the symbolic, that was masterful. His way of making a huge statement with a tiny case, that was really something to me. It was like having a flashlight in a cave. We were all inching along in the dark, hoping we were going forward and not in circles, and then Julian would shine the light and we'd see a piece of the cave. It might be exactly like the miles and miles we'd already covered, but suddenly we'd see it.'' He smiled sadly. ''We'd see what we'd done and why we'd done it.''

''You'd see a small case, Clement. Handled in a splashy way guaranteed to send some poor client to jail.''

"Maybe that's what *you*'d see. I'd see commitment—the client's commitment, our commitment. I'd see continuity. Progress."

We might as well have known a different man.

"When Julian died, I couldn't imagine inching through the cave in the dark alone," Clement concluded. "Even though his style was not my style, I needed him to make me feel good about the way I did things. Because for every little thing he did so publicly, I knew I was doing five dozen things quietly."

"And you didn't resent him getting all the attention and the credit?"

"Why should I? I told you, I was in it for the work. The more work I did, the better I felt. And the more credit Julian got, the more worthwhile the work seemed to me." He paused, eyes glittering. "You might ask yourself whether you don't have the same kind of relationship with your parents that I had with Julian."

"Symbiotic?" I shook my head. "I'm not into symbols."

"Oh, but they don't shine their lights on symbols—that's what they used to hire Julian to do. If I had to pick out the thing about your parents that makes them who they are, that keeps them active, it would be heart. Heart." He tapped his chest. "They do what they do because they feel it. They feel a sincere love for the people they try to help."

I recalled my last visit with them. "Are they in some kind of trouble again, Clement? Do you know?" It would be less painful to believe that than to believe they'd colluded with Edward Hershey.

"Well . . ." He suddenly looked like a lawyer—an expressionless version of himself, a police artist's rendition. "I think they may be trying to help someone out." Seeing my alarm, he added, "In a purely legal way."

"It's not Edward Hershey, is it?"

He froze for a moment, then slowly shook his head. "No, it isn't." A moment later: "Really, Willa, it's purely legal—almost sanctioned. Believe me. They're just trying to help someone."

Trying to help someone. I thought about their years in the Peace Corps in dusty African villages. Salvadoran ladies with broods of babies camping in what had once been my bedroom. Mother's tear-stained letters to Texas prisoners.

Heart. I could admire it—did admire it—when it didn't negate caution, didn't negate sense.

"If you're saying I should do something . . ."

"Right now, just thinking about all this is probably enough." He smiled a toothy smile. "You'll come out in the right place."

It would have been nice, in a pop-psych way, to think so. But I didn't see any other reason to believe it.

I stood, extending my hand. Clement took it, rising and stepping toward me so that the handshake became an embrace.

"I care about you," he said.

I felt a hot flood of gratitude. I'd gotten precious few phone calls in L.A.—not many of my lefty friends wanted to talk to corporate lawyers. (Unfortunately for my social life, I felt the same way.) But Clement had phoned me. He'd gotten me my job. He was trying to get me my next one.

I wanted to please him, be more like him.

At that moment, if he'd been the Wizard of Oz, I'd have asked him for a (bleeding) heart.

Since he wasn't, I went home and got stoned instead.

28

DON SURGELATO STOOD in my doorway. Handsome, with his broken nose and thinning curls, his cherubic lips and cleft chin.

I was still in my work clothes; mostly dressed, in stocking feet. He was dressed for work, too; tidy blue suit, blue tie. (What is it about George Bush and blue ties?)

Woolly-brained and cranky, I was able to suppress my sexual desire. But I didn't press my luck. I didn't look at him too closely. I didn't stand near enough to smell his cologne.

I said, "I just got home from work." Via Clement's.

"I'm still at work," he replied sourly. "Can I come in, please." It wasn't a question.

I hesitated. Whatever he wanted to talk about, I didn't want to hear it. I'd been stupid. I'd reached out to a married man and I'd been slapped back. The rejection was complete; it didn't require the personal touch.

"This is business," he said. "You knew Margarita Delacort, didn't you?"

Knew.

I felt my hands slide into my hair. I visualized her on the canvas cushions of her porch loveseat. I could almost hear her voice, flattened by an excess of emotion.

She'd confided in me, held my interest, engaged my emotions. I hadn't thought about it, hadn't articulated it, but I liked her.

It's not possible for anyone else I like to die. Not possible.

I turned away and walked to the window. Looked out at streetcar wires scribbled over my view of drab apartments in dim lamplight. *Jump and don't find out and don't know.*

People can't keep dying around me. I can't get to know people and have them die. They just can't do that.

I turned again to face him. "No one in L.A. died."

He winced.

"My therapist always wanted me to talk about it," I heard myself blither. "About the others. Julian. That's one of the reasons I left L.A. I didn't want to talk about it. I didn't want to think about it. I wanted it to be officially over."

He sighed, stepping in and closing the door behind him. "You'll be okay," he said. "But it's not over. We've got to talk about Margarita Delacort."

I backed up till I could feel the window on my back, the sill against my thigh.

"Rita Delacort is okay," I insisted. "I saw her. She told me about her mother-in-law. Her husbands. Edward." I reached out, as if to relay meaning through my arms. "I like her. She's fine. It's her dog that's sick."

He watched me, his face composed into a heavy-lidded

mask. "This is my job," he said. "This is what I do. I appear at times like this."

"We talked. She has two children."

"They're all right."

"Not if she isn't." I pressed my back to the glass pane.

"She isn't. She was cut down by an automatic rifle today— a machine gun, in popular parlance. In the yard of her house on the summit of the Santa Cruz Mountains. You were there recently. That's what her husband says."

You run away from some things. Even if it means leaving a city, more than one city. Leaving a therapist. Leaving a political philosophy. You run and you hope the things don't catch you. You move. You hole up. You drink. You smoke pot.

"Which is not my jurisdiction," he pointed out. "Except that I helped hook Margarita Delacort into the FBI's witness protection program. Almost twenty years ago, when I was in uniform." A wistful look. "And green in judgment."

"Who was she?"

"No."

"Who was she being protected from?"

An elaborate Italian shrug.

"You won't tell me?"

"I can't tell you. They're the focus of our investigation. Us and Santa Cruz County. And the feds." His face looked haggard, older than I remembered.

You're not happy with your wife, I thought. For all your talk about loyalty and loneliness, I've never heard you say you love her. I've never heard you say you're happy.

"You want me to tell you how I know Rita Delacort."

"Yes."

"Okay. Sit down. I— Can I make coffee, I'd like coffee."

"Go ahead."

I felt my legs propel me into the kitchen. They didn't feel

like my legs, they felt like ill-fitting appliances. I went through the motions: I put on water, I filled the cone filter.

Yes, I'd known Rita Delacort.

And Bob LeVoq. Jim Zissner. Julian Warneke. Greg Parker. Susan Green.

I was still standing there when Don pushed through the door. He made a rumbling sound that I took for exasperation. I mopped tears with my sleeve, stammered an apology.

He pulled me into an embrace, and I clung to him. A while, I think.

I felt the character of the embrace begin to change, change as my focus changed: the crispness of his hair against my temple, the warmth of his cheek, the press of muscle through his jacket, the smell of soap, shampoo, sidestream cigarette smoke. He was holding me, not just comforting me.

Then his arms slid off me like melting ice. His voice was low, grim. "This isn't the sixties, the seventies, where you feel a certain way and you go for it—'if it feels good, do it.'"

I turned away, embarrassed by the nakedness of my (temporally incorrect) desire.

The kettle was boiling. I forced myself to continue making coffee.

Against a background of clattering crockery, he added, "Don't you get it, Willa?"

That sex is risky, love unprofessional? Control, good sense, safety. Marriage to an old sweetheart. The nineties.

He stood behind me, shuffling, uttering a disjointed syllable and then stopping.

The coffee ritual got me through the next few minutes. Then, avoiding his eye, I led him into the living room.

I sat stiffly. I told the lieutenant how I'd come to meet Rita Delacort. Related my conversations with her.

I asked him again who she really was and what the witness protection program had protected her from.

He looked at me, really looked, eyes liquid, corners of his mouth pinched. But he didn't tell me much. Only that Rita Delacort had testified in a court case in exchange for immunity from prosecution. That her testimony had created a level of risk ultimately forcing her to assume a new identity.

"Our assumption is that the false identity was pierced," he concluded. "The program can't provide continuing security. I understand she had a guard dog."

"He was sick."

"Dead. He was poisoned."

"And someone broke into Edward Hershey's house, beat him up. She'd been staying there."

"Yes. We know about that."

"But she wasn't there that night?"

Surgelato shook his head.

"You all know who she was—really was. If you don't tell me, I'll wonder about it and worry about it and be afraid I had something to do with her death."

He scowled. Finally raised both palms. "That's not how we do things."

We hide behind our professionalism. All of us do, if we've sacrificed enough for it. It protects us. It spares us the pain of moral debate.

I understood.

I wasn't worth breaking the rules for.

29

"PLEASE TELL ME who she was."

Philip Delacort blinked at me. He stood in the doorway of his mountain home, his cheeks sunk in a pale sheen, his shoulders narrowed with knotted tension. From some corner of the house came the manic theme of television cartoons.

He glanced over his shoulder, glanced back at me. He started to say something, shook his head, threw up his hands. Finally, he stepped back to let me in. I was glad to leave the porch, the redwood loveseat vanishing from my peripheral vision.

His house was a miracle of engineering—so much glass you had to wonder what held the roof up. He must have kept a few glaziers busy after the earthquake.

I followed him into a room dominated by a stone fireplace with fat leather chairs grouped around it. In spite of a cold, undisturbed look, it was a house for which I'd have forgiven a husband almost anything.

Delacort sat on the edge of a chair, its leather cushion sighing. "What are you doing here?"

"I know your wife was in the witness protection program." Is that what Don had called it?

I was startled to see Delacort grow paler. "I want to know who she really was."

He relaxed his spine, shoulders sagging into the chair back. The bad posture made him look collegiate, vulnerable.

"She was born Christine Rice."

The name meant nothing to me. "What did she do? Why was she in the program?"

"She phoned the police." He covered his eyes with his hand. His skin was dry and red, the nails well tended.

I listened to distant cartoon noises, somebody getting bonked. Delacort's children, assuming they watched, did not laugh.

Delacort remained slumped in the chair, face hidden behind chafed knuckles.

I felt cruel doing this to him. Shaky doing it to myself. The house felt haunted. Damn Surgelato, anyway. He could have told me; saved me a two-hour car trip on a foggy morning.

"I'm sorry if I seem nosy, but . . ." But what? But I woke up and smoked a joint and drove the cliffs of the coast highway stoned. I've never done that before. I did it even though I know it's stupid. Even though it scared me. Because it's too horrible that someone else I know has been murdered. "Do you have any coffee?"

He remained motionless, didn't seem to hear. For a second, I thought he might have died behind those red knuckles.

"Christine was a member of an armed cadre. The cadre kidnapped a baby—"

"Not Highway Sixty-one? The industrialist's baby?"

"Yes."

Highway 61. As in Harry Prough's disastrous conspiracy trial.

I remembered Rita Delacort's—Christine Rice's—reaction last Saturday when I mentioned Harry Prough's name. When I mentioned Prough was opposing counsel in her husband's securities fraud case. Oh, no, she'd said. Oh, no. And I hadn't even wondered why.

"They kidnapped the baby of Dow Chemical's vice president," Delacort continued, "or maybe it was Du Pont. Hunh." He sounded mildly surprised to have forgotten this detail. "Because the company manufactured napalm." His voice was tired, nonjudgmental. "They brought the baby to Rita's—Chris's—house."

The story was familiar, even if the name wasn't. "She turned them in." No wonder she'd harped so much on security, on feeling safe with her dogs, with Delacort.

His hand dropped from his face. His blue eyes were serene, his face wiped clean of emotion. "She didn't think they'd hurt the baby, but she wasn't sure. There was some talk about burning it—symbolic of napalm, you know? They were her friends, her comrades, but she wasn't sure—one or two of them, she wasn't completely sure about. She freaked out and went to the police. Testified against them—friends, like I said. She's still . . . before she died, she still wasn't sure she'd done the right thing. But the FBI gave her a new identity. After a while. I met her my last year of law school; she worked in the library. Flunky stuff, shelving. She kept a low profile—a lot of politicos in the Bay Area. When I got a job in San Jose, we figured it would be okay." A listless wave of the arm. "Mountain house. Quiet life." His gaze drifted to a wall of windows overlooking his terraced garden. "But she got restless. She got tired of me. Flaming radical past and all that."

The corners of his mouth crimped, his chin began to knot. He repeated, "She got tired of me. I'm not a very interesting guy; my life is my career. Not very glamorous—your basic sellout kind of career, you know. But what could I do? I couldn't work with leftists, people who might recognize her."

He fixed me with bright eyes, begging me to agree that he'd trodden a dull path purely for his wife's sake. That it wasn't his choice, wasn't his fault he'd turned into one more perfect haircut with a wine cellar.

"Harry Prough, for instance, he defended Highway Sixty-one. Sure, I'd have liked to do the kind of work he does—high profile, cutting edge—but . . . but I couldn't do it without meeting him socially, without my wife meeting him. He'd have recognized her in a second. Any left-wing lawyer might have recognized her—might have seen her testify. So . . ." A shrug.

At least I admitted I'd sold out for money. I'd sold out for a new car and new furniture. From lefty to catalog shopper; my choice.

"Highway Sixty-one—how many of those people are out of jail now?"

"Most of them—hell, I've seen one in the Federal Building elevator. But how would they know Rita was Chris?" Delacort's tone approached a whine. "How would they know where she lived? She didn't go up to the city much. She didn't even go into Santa Cruz much." He straightened, arching his back. "Unless she and Hershey . . . Well, face it. What did I know about her habits anymore? I tried to keep her careful. Who knows what she did when I wasn't with her."

"Edward Hershey knew about this."

Something about my statement smoothed the hurt off Delacort's face. The flicker of vulnerability—of humanity—was quenched by practiced composure. He looked like a lawyer again.

"Maybe not. My wife wasn't in the habit of mentioning it. Even if she hadn't been at risk, her feelings were unresolved. She didn't like to talk about it, even with me. Especially after she had children of her own."

Children of her own, not their own. Would he abandon the children to television and au pairs now? Remain immersed in the career that made him dull?

"She got pregnant very young. Decided under pressure from her family to put the baby up for adoption. She felt very guilty about it—it was a major factor in her turning Highway Sixty-one in. Their threats against the vice president's baby."

"Edward Hershey knew the whole story." I remembered what she'd said about an early affair with him, moving in with him later when things got rough. After the Highway 61 trial, that's what she'd meant.

I realized that my parents knew the whole story, too.

That's why they allowed Edward to "run into" me outside their apartment. He wanted me to do a favor for a radical in distress. Of course my parents agreed to help him. Of course they invited him in. It wasn't kismet, it was conspiracy.

But what exactly had I done for Edward? What exactly had I done for Christine/Rita?

30

IT WAS UNPROFESSIONAL of me to roll into work in the late afternoon, still slightly stoned. If I hadn't already known that, it would have been plain to read in George McLeod's reaction.

He looked up from a trial transcript. His brows sank and his lips vanished between clipped beard and mustache. "Oh, good work." His sarcasm was as subtle as an eighth grader's. He tossed his pencil down. "Nice of you to call and let us know you'll be late."

"It doesn't matter. I'm quitting again."

He shook his head, his mouth opening like a carp's. "You can't quit a job you just started!"

"Because it's bad for my résumé?"

"No! Well, yes, obviously it is. But it's unprofessional. Very unprofessional."

I waited to feel something. He'd flung at me the very reproof with which I'd excoriated myself the last time I quit. But I stared at him, at his livid face and clenched fists, and I felt nothing. Yes, it would be unprofessional to quit again; and yes, I had devoted years of my life to becoming and behaving like a professional.

"I've been thinking, George, driving up the coast highway wondering what it is I did for Edward Hershey. I mean, he went to all the trouble of recruiting my parents—"

"Or don't you give a damn?" George leaped to his feet. "Don't you give a damn how many résumés the judge and I looked at before hiring you? Two hundred, probably. We must have interviewed fifteen candidates. We actually picked someone else. We disappointed a very sharp woman from Harvard so you could waltz in late today and act like, Oh, gee, I don't need this piddly job anyway."

"My parents made sure Hershey had a chance to talk to me, made sure he had a chance to ask me his favor. So obviously the whole thing revolves around the favor. And since it wasn't anything much, it has to be the end result that's important. It has to be the fact that Shanna disqualified himself."

"You feel you're entitled to have your little crises, right, and the hell with the judge. The hell with his work, which is damned important. Damned important!" He looked ready to knock me down if I disagreed.

"What bothers me is, how did Hershey know the judge would disqualify himself? Because the judge really, on the surface, didn't have to. According to *Federal Procedure*."

"You come here and act like you're killing time till you decide what you really want to do. Like your law degree's some kind of albatross. Like you're some big martyr because you spent a year at a big L.A. firm. Well, a year's nothing!'' he opined. ''Nothing! You're supposed to be in this for the long haul!''

He took a few angry strides toward me.

I hate angry men in my face. ''In what, George? What am I *in* that deserves my undivided and abject loyalty?''

I get sick of being told I have to give my whole self to something transcendently important, be it movement politics or a long-haul career. As if loyalty is some monolithic thing, some all-or-nothing thing divorced from circumstance.

George backed off, sat down. ''Is it the drugs?''

''What?''

''You're a drug addict, are you not?'' He looked at me, his eyes narrowing.

''No!'' He'd smelled a little pot in my living room—what kind of sheltered Republican would conclude from that that I'm a drug addict? ''No, I'm not.'' The second time with less conviction. I was stoned now. Stoned at work.

I sat, too. ''Hand me your *Federal Procedure*, George.''

He scowled at me. I finally had to stand, stretch, pluck it off his desk myself.

Under his nimbus gaze, I opened the book to the still-marked section I'd read yesterday, the section informing me that Harry Prough could have filed an affidavit and avoided his contempt arrest.

I flipped forward to the other section George had marked. Section 455, circumstances under which judges must disqualify themselves.

It was a detailed section, a page of tiny print. But no surprises: judges must disqualify themselves if their impartiality may reasonably be questioned, if they are biased about a party, if they have personal facts about a case, if they have a financial or personal interest in the outcome, if their spouses, children or others "within a third degree of relationship" are parties to the action or would be affected by the outcome.

Not a thing about judges' clerks having private, unrelated talks with parties' lawyers.

I handed the book back to George, marking the place with my finger. He failed to take the hint, so I leaned closer and opened it in front of him.

"You mentioned this section yesterday," I reminded him. "Harry Prough cited it."

George skimmed it. Though I wouldn't have thought it possible, his expression grew more sour. "You're obsessed with Judge Shanna disqualifying himself. What's the big deal? He might have been a little overscrupulous but—"

"Not overscrupulous, just scrupulous. He had to disqualify himself, and the reason is in there."

"Of course it's in there. I mean, not specifically, but maybe he thought . . ." He scanned the section again. "I don't know what he thought. But he wasn't picking on you personally; you're blowing this all out of—"

"He didn't give the real reason for disqualifying himself. He didn't have to because I was his pretext. His straw clerk."

"What are you talking about?"

"He set me up, George. Shanna set me up."

With a little help from my friends.

31

I FOUND THE judge reading the *Examiner*. He looked startled when I walked in without knocking. He put the paper aside and I could see the headline in the Metro section: FEDERAL JUDGE ACCUSED OF BIAS. I felt a surge of glee; the papers were trying Rondi, not Prough.

"You and Clement Kerrey are good friends." I tapped his triple portrait of Jimmy Carter. Dust rose from the felt backing.

Judge Shanna was pale under his freckles. Midday brightness poured through the glass wall, spotlighting uncharacteristic blemishes on his chin and forehead. The room smelled of hot sun on old carpet.

"Yes." His voice was bland and ungoaded. "From the presidential campaign."

"He's your lawyer. You go to him for advice."

His face was as blank as Delacort's. I wondered if it was an occupational hazard. I wondered if my lawyer mask was as characterless as theirs.

"When I need personal legal advice, yes, I go to Clement."

"You told him you couldn't hear a case tried by Philip Delacort." He barely blinked when I uttered the name. "Because of what it says in *Federal Procedure*."

" 'Within a third degree of relationship,' " he quoted.

If he were related to Delacort, he could have said so.

"Christine Rice was in the witness protection program."

She was also a relative of Judge Shanna's, otherwise none of this made sense. Otherwise Shanna would not have felt compelled to disqualify himself from a case argued by her husband.

The problem was, how could he—scrupulous jurist— reconcile this ethical mandate with the state-imposed obligation to conceal the identity of a government witness? How could he disqualify himself and still maintain the silence necessary to ensure her anonymity?

"You told Clement you couldn't try a case argued by her husband. But you couldn't reveal her identity, either. You'd discussed it with Delacort and decided you needed some kind of pretext. For opposing counsel's sake. For Harry Prough's sake."

The judge bracketed his chin between his thumb and forefinger, sighing. "If it had been anyone other than Harry . . ." Harry, who'd defended Christine Rice's comrades. "It's funny how these things lie dormant for so long, and then suddenly everywhere you turn . . ."

Everywhere you turn?

"Luckily, I got wind of the fact that the state planned to file charges against Tom Rugieri."

Tom Rugieri, on whose behalf I'd recently written a stirring defense of the Fourth Amendment (before the prosecution saved some resources and moved to dismiss the case before Judge Shanna). Tom Rugieri, formerly of Highway 61.

Jesus, why hadn't I thought of him before? Maybe I *was* smoking too much pot.

The name Christine Rice had meant nothing to me, but Chris Rugieri—the Judas of Highway 61. I remembered Chris Rugieri. A redhead back then. Chris Rugieri, now I remembered her.

The wife of Tom Rugieri. The first time I met Rita, she'd referred to someone named Tom; said she'd seen him, been to his hearing. God, what if it was Rita Delacort in the Federal Building corridor with Don and me after Rugieri's hearing? Rita in a blond wig, hoping to catch an inconspicuous glimpse of her first husband.

The judge continued, ''I felt reasonably confident the prosecution would move to dismiss the federal action against Rugieri. For the reasons Mr. Prough outlined.''

For the sleaziest possible reasons, in fact. Reasons another federal judge—a disinterested judge—might have challenged.

I waited for him to say more, but he just sat there, thumb tracing his jawline. My fingers itched to seize his tie, to pull him forward and make him apologize for lying to me, make him beg my forgiveness.

''Clement knew Chris Rugieri. Or you introduced them.''

Shanna nodded slightly, his shoulders rounding.

''And Edward Hershey's name came up. Chris Rugieri mentioned Edward Hershey.''

''No, we left Christine out of it. It was Delacort who suggested Hershey. As a possible resource, a detective in on the secret, should we need one. It's ironic. I understand she moved in with Mr. Hershey a short time later.''

I wondered what story Hershey would have used to get me to talk to Delacort if she hadn't.

''We were at our wits' end, Clement and Delacort and I, trying to resolve the dilemma.''

Clement knew about me and Edward Hershey. He'd seen us together when Edward first joined me in San Francisco. He'd seen us squabbling years later at Julian Warneke's wake. ''Was this before or after you hired me?''

He leaned back, squinting out at the cold blue sky. ''Before.''

So Clement's excited phone call to me, urging me to apply for a last-minute clerkship— ''You hired me just to be your excuse.''

''You were qualified.''

Overqualified; too experienced, too long out of law school to be a judge's lapdog. In the ordinary course of things, Shanna would have offered the job to someone fresher, more gung ho. Someone like George.

''Clement told Edward to get me over to Delacort's house. That's what you hired me to do.''

''My preference''—the judge spread his palms—''would have been to approach you with this directly and appeal to your humanitarianism.''

''Yes, well.'' Clement had seen my cynicism close up. Maybe he wasn't so sure of my humanitarianism. Maybe that's what dinner at my parents' house had been about. Maybe it had been a test; maybe the group had concluded I was no longer a caring and sensitive lefty, no longer a good sport. ''I guess Clement knew that if it came to this—to my finding out after the fact—I'd keep my mouth shut.''

No one would ever question Judge Shanna's disqualification, not unless I raised a stink. Investigators assigned to the

Rugieri case would not think it relevant, even if they heard about it; they would believe it stemmed from my misconduct. The judge's reputation would remain untarnished. And I'd half-considered leaping off a bridge.

"Understand, Willa." His deep voice was shaded with avuncular concern. "My niece's life was in danger. I could neither hear her husband's case nor reveal my actual reason for disqualifying myself. Clement and I felt, on balance, that the risk to Christine outweighed whatever discomfiture you might feel at having—inadvertently!—done something technically inappropriate."

And yet, for all his pallor and soft speech, Michael Shanna did not seem to mourn Christine Rice Rugieri. He recalled her as a judicial quandary, a moral abstraction like the Fourth Amendment.

"In the final analysis, it was all for nothing. You didn't save your niece. She was killed anyway." And you put me through hell when I might have helped of my own free will.

He drew back, as far back as he could go without tipping his chair. "Having done what we could to protect her identity—"

"Oh, spare me!" I knocked down the triple portrait of Carter. "George is always calling you results oriented, but it's not true. You're process oriented. You and the whole fucking Left. We never manage to save the targets of our beneficence, do we; we just like the feeling of trying. And we're so blind to each other in the process, so cavalier in our rush to do good—" That it's a wonder more of us don't end up on some bridge, poised to jump.

But maybe that wasn't fair. When Clement Kerrey's heart bled to save Christine Rugieri—when he enlisted my parents and my ex-lover to deceive me on behalf of my employer—he couldn't have guessed I'd quit my job, couldn't have guessed I'd take it so hard.

Maybe it wasn't fair to blame him, to blame my parents. But I did. I blamed them for deciding without sufficient information that deceiving me would serve the greater good. I blamed them for deciding I was just the unimportant means to a worthy end.

I agreed the end was paramount. But couldn't they have trusted my instincts enough to recruit me instead of use me? Working a year for a corporate firm didn't make me Margaret Thatcher, for godsake.

I blamed myself, too, for going out of my way to put my trust—in Clement, the judge, my parents—to the test. Trust no one: my worst fear confirmed.

32

I ELBOWED MY way into an already-full elevator. A Hispanic family ruffled the curls of a sullen teenager, embracing him, weeping over him. The boy looked embarrassed, enduring the fuss. From the back of the elevator a snide voice said, "Rondi let him off with probation. Can you believe it?"

It was Harry Prough, hair rumpled, a day's growth on his cheeks. A business-suited clerk frowned crankily in his direction, jostled herself a little farther from him.

"His hearing was right before mine," Prough continued. "Had a character letter from some asshole Republican in the governor's office. That's what it takes these days—forget a paltry little thing like the Bill of Rights."

A squat old woman sputtered, "Good boy, never trouble."

It shocked me to see Prough out of jail. Even I could have held on to my pride longer than one day. Even I could have waited one more day to kiss Rondi's hem.

As the elevator doors opened, all I could think to say was, "You should be in jail."

I left him with that uncharitable thought.

33

I KEPT MY curtains closed, my door locked, my phone off the hook. I smoked pot.

So okay, dignity, sobriety, detachment—that would have been the laudable response. But why display poise when there's no one around to appreciate it? It's like wearing lace teddies at home alone.

Not that I had to be alone. At dinnertime, my parents came upstairs and rapped on my door. I could hear them talking in the corridor—I knew it was them. I remained on the couch, watching smoke from the joint curl around my fingers.

I could hear Mother shuffle and kibbitz while my father told the closed door that he'd talked to Clement, who'd talked to Shanna; and that they all knew in my heart I understood. He relied on me to see that sometimes protecting the collective and metaphoric nest meant turning your (metaphoric) back on your own chick.

I heard Mother add, "She can't call us knee-jerk this time. It was a radical group we were worried about."

"Clement put it to us this way," my father continued. "The judge felt he had to withdraw from the case, and if he couldn't find some excuse, he'd have to give the real reason. The woman's identity would be revealed and her life would be in danger."

"We wanted to tell you, Baby, really. But Edward said the fewer people who knew, the safer she was. We were trying to save a life," Mother concluded. "Help someone who needed our help."

Help someone. Not just words to them. My whole childhood we'd had refugees camped on the couch, petitions spread across the coffee table, strike relief funds in stacked coffee cans. No matter how broke my parents were or how bare their pantry was, the neighborhood homeless could count on a meal at our house.

That's who my parents were. I understood that. I admired that. (Didn't they realize I admired that?)

But I didn't open the door.

Finally, they went away.

Then Harry Prough came. He pounded on the door, announcing himself like I should pull out trumpets and play something imperial.

He said, "Open the fucking door. I know who killed Chris Rugieri. It's my fault and I feel like hell, and you're going to help me fix things."

I sat there staring at the door. I don't fix things when I'm stoned. I sit on the couch.

"Goddam it!" Prough rattled the doorknob. "I didn't kowtow to Rondi just to stand here waiting for you to stop being a princess."

So why did he kowtow?

"Open the door."

My hero. Even I had greater courage of my convictions. Even I could have put up with more than twenty-four hours. But then, I didn't have four years of traumatic prison memories. And I had greater reason to dislike Rondi.

I wavered. I would need a job soon, and Prough could provide one.

But right now, the idea of practicing law appalled me.

"I'm not dinky-donking around, Willa! I know who killed Chris Rugieri. And I know why—because I didn't think this fucking thing through. Because I shot my mouth off."

To Tom Rugieri? "Why are you telling me this?"

"Yeah, okay, it sounds a little silly when I say it. But I'm not kidding."

I stood shakily. Alone in the dark room, I felt almost invisible. Incorporeal.

"Come on," he coaxed. "Let me in."

I'd have opened the door to Julian Warneke's killer, opened it without a second thought. I'd have opened the door to Susan Green's killer. To Bob LeVoq's killer.

Today I wouldn't open the door to anyone. Not anyone. Not my own parents.

"Look," he pleaded, "I can't be shouting about this in your hallway. It was a client, okay? *Not* who you're thinking! Rugieri's in jail. They busted him on the state charge."

Did he mean it? Not Tom Rugieri?

"It was a plaintiff in my class action—someone I didn't realize was linked to Highway Sixty-one. I mouthed off about Shanna's disqualification, and the client thought it through. It's no secret Shanna is Chris Rugieri's uncle, you know. Obviously my client got it that Shanna's so-called reason for disqualification was horseshit."

Shanna's so-called reason—I had provided that information. If Prough was saying I'd tipped the domino leading to Rita Delacort's murder, I didn't want to hear it. Couldn't stand to hear it.

"Client thought faster than I did," Prough continued. "Came up with Delacort. That Chris Rugieri must be connected with opposing counsel in that case."

A long silence.

"It's my fucking fault," he concluded. "For bitching about the disqualification. For blurting out my skepticism." A short pause. "Shit."

I could almost hear my therapist saying no, you can't control other people's behavior, you have to let go of responsibility for actions over which you have no control. Therapists can get away with saying things like that. But no one else believes them.

"Who's the client?"

"Fuck—if you think I'm going to tell a closed door—We're talking about my client. You could have a tape recorder in there. I'll tell you face to face."

"No."

"I can't just tell you. I have to know you're alone, not wired. Godsake, open the door."

Sure. Fluttering my lashes like a B-movie bimbo.

"Come on. In all seriousness, I have a plan."

"A plan." It came out way on the other side of snide.

"Okay granted, it sounds a little *Scaramouche*. But a woman's dead. It's my fault. I don't want them hassling Tom Rugieri—he's got nothing to do with this. And I'm limited in what I can do. I need you. I need your help."

Another long silence. "You might as well, Willa. You're going to try the class action with me, aren't you?"

A renewal of the job offer. Talk about going for the soft underbelly.

"Can I be blunt, Harry?"

"Yes."

"I don't trust you." I don't trust anyone. I wish I never had.

I waited for some response. Waited what seemed several minutes. Finally I clicked on a light, an art deco pole lamp that had looked prettier in the catalog than in my living room.

There was a file folder on the floor near my door, part of it still on the other side. I approached it cautiously.

"Harry?" I said.

"Yeah?"

"Go away."

I bent to pick up the file. It was unlabeled. I opened it and found a list of the plaintiffs in Prough's class action.

I read through it.

Came to a name I recognized.

My God. He couldn't mean that person. He couldn't.

34

TWO YEARS AGO an arrest warrant issued in the murder of Julian Warneke. It had my name on it. I had just eluded Julian's killer, barely avoided being one more gory puddle on Julian's office carpet. I had cowered on a window ledge, in fact; freezing, panicking, certain I would not survive. Tempted to jump; deny; escape.

Later I'd wandered the streets, awakening to my parents' complicity—well intentioned, of course; kindly meant, of course. Wholly unrelated to the murder, and yet criminal. Complicity certain to send them to prison if I revealed the identity of Julian's killer.

But I did reveal it. I revealed it in the back of Don Surgelato's government car, the one he'd driven to my parents' house to arrest me. He could have sent a "team," he'd told me. But he'd come himself. He'd come to tell me he didn't believe in my guilt. He'd come to tell me he'd do anything to help me. If I'd only trust him. Tell him the truth.

And ratlike, I'd pressed the lever. Crazy about him in a way that smacked of teenage rebellion. A cop.

I'd trusted him with my parents' freedom. All that it meant to me.

And he'd come through. He'd protected them the only way anyone could protect them, by killing Julian's murderer. Guaranteeing silence.

Since then, I'd thought about Don Surgelato every night. Every night I'd burrowed into my pillow, giving it his features. Trying to recall the scent of his cologne. Trying to wish him into my arms.

Now and then, I'd gone out on a limb; gone to his house or called him or met him for coffee. Now and then, I'd let myself see how one-sided it was. Let him push me away.

It was almost worth the resulting pain. Seeing him was almost worth it.

That's what I told myself when I rang his doorbell that night.

I was still telling myself that when his wife answered.

Tina Surgelato wore a belted velour robe, floor length, smoky purple. Her black hair was short this year, punky, spiky. Tamed by a sedately forty-fiveish face, mostly unwrinkled, well creamed around pretty green eyes. Bee-stung lips. Busty. Tall. Striking in ways I wasn't. I looked up at her and felt colorless, inconsequential, pinched.

I said, "Is the lieutenant home?"

She seemed to be trying not to frown. Tiny lines appeared between her brows, vanished, appeared again. The skin there glistened.

"No," she said.

"Good. I'd like to talk to you."

She shook her head. "No. Talk to him. He'll tell me about it if he wants to. It's his business."

His business? God, did she think I was sleeping with him? I had to give her points for dignity.

"It's not what you think." Behind her, thickly carpeted stairs rose to a second-floor living room. I remembered it from my one and only other visit. Comfortable furniture, good watercolors. A whole house in North Beach. Bought with family money. Italo-American Bank money.

Her cheeks flamed with color. She looked beautiful. A little middle-aged, a little gaudy. A little too primped, too creamed, too purple, too lush. But beautiful.

"I don't want to talk to you. I know you've been calling Don. I know you've been meeting him."

"No. Not really."

"I'm not going to start making him account for his time! I'm not nineteen anymore, I won't go through that again." She ran a long-nailed hand through her moussed hair.

He had described her as brittle. And last time I'd seen her, she'd been wrapped in false laughter. Splashing desperate glances around the room. Not today.

"I'm not Don's parent. If he's been, if he's started—"

"He hasn't. Please let me talk to you." I held up the file folder Harry Prough had pushed under my door. "It's about a legal matter. Please."

She expelled her breath, eyes closed. Controlling herself. Spine so straight in her majestic purple. She must be almost as tall as Don. Maybe it's easier for tall people to display poise.

She turned and began climbing the stairs. I closed the door and followed her.

The living room was rearranged. No more groupings of comfortable chairs. It was uncluttered space now, furniture

against the walls, walls lined with cherrywood bookcases
and entertainment centers. The watercolors remained, boats
becalmed on tranquil bay. Through vertical blinds, I could
see city lights winking.

She sighed, sitting on the arm of a white sofa.

I sat opposite her on a matching chair, the width of the big
room between us.

"You're a named plaintiff in a class action suit," I said.
Mrs. Don Surgelato, the last name on Prough's sheet; penned
onto a typed list. "Your lawyer, Harry Prough, he complained to you about the judge in that suit disqualifying himself." I watched her. "Didn't he?"

Her cheeks spotted red. High contrast with her black hair
and white skin. Too much, almost. Almost feverish. "Don
tells me about it when he sees you. He tells me you're troubled, that you have been since those murders. That you turn
to him because of his authority role. His parental role."

It would have hurt less if she'd slapped me.

"I'm a licensed therapist now," she said. "I know this is
hard for you to hear from me, but have you considered talking to someone?" A flicker of annoyance. "Someone other
than Don."

He'd told me years ago his wife was in college, getting a
Ph.D. in psychology. I shouldn't have been so surprised.

"Because," she continued, "I've got to tell you, I've never
heard of Harry Prough. I've never been involved in a lawsuit
in my life."

I felt the file folder flutter in my fingers. I looked down at
it, almost afraid to open it. What if her name wasn't there,
after all? What if I'd imagined it? Knowing it was almost
certain she had no motive, no opportunity, no idea who Chris
Rugieri was. What if I wanted her to be the killer? Just to get
her away from him.

"Will you look at this?" I heard myself say. Tell me I'm not hallucinating.

I stretched my arm out, offering the folder.

I focused all my attention on the folder, not wanting to look at her face. I watched her hand take it. I saw it framed in the luxuriant velour of her lap. I watched it open, I watched her polished fingernail scroll down the list. I watched it stop.

"I never go by 'Mrs. Don,' " she said. "My mother-in-law used to."

I looked at her face. She was frowning, oblivious to the creamed wrinkles.

"But she died last year."

35

THE DOWNSTAIRS SECURITY guard recognized me, waving me behind him so I didn't have to stand in line at the electronic metal detector. The upstairs guard recognized me, too; didn't blink an eye when I asked to be master-keyed into Shanna's clerks' office.

I switched on the overhead lights, fancying that I could detect purple tones in the bright fluorescence, that I could track its infinitesimally rapid winking. Maybe I was just tired.

Too tired to be here. Too paranoid to go home. Except I didn't know where else to go.

Maybe to my parents' flat. They would welcome me, be grateful that I'd come. That counted for something, even if I was too angry to go there now. Still angry that they'd used me as a tool toward a desirable end. (But yes, I understood why they might doubt my willingness to be unprofessional for a good cause. I hadn't told them how I'd felt about working for Wailes, Roth. I'd let them see my cynicism but not my confusion.)

I'd considered going to Clement Kerrey's house—I was in the habit of being grateful for his friendship. But he'd engineered this. I'd have to find other friends. Friends as kind. Friends more honest. Sometime, somehow.

I phoned Edward Hershey. Unfinished business.

He answered on the third ring, a little out of breath, his voice low. Maybe purposely. A sexy telephone voice.

"Edward," I said. Just that one word. It was enough of an accusation.

"Willa?" A bristle of guilt, maybe fear.

"You lied to me, you son of a bitch. You looked me right in the eye and lied to me."

A brief silence. "A little hard for me to get choked up about that right now."

"Oh, yeah?" I could hear the whine of hysteria in my voice.

"Look, I'm sorry. But what was I supposed to do? I couldn't tell you. There was too much at stake. A friend's life, her *life*— It's not that I wanted to lie to you, but . . . Fuck, how could I be concerned about anything except—"

"I don't want to hear it." So why did I call? Still wanting to believe he was a pal? Wanting to believe a former lover wouldn't let me down? "Thanks for the fucking vote of confidence."

"Willa, Jesus, it was for—"

"The greater good? Fuck that. What do you know about the greater good?"

"I was going to say, for a friend. To save a life." A choking sound, followed by an almost inaudible keening. He was crying.

Maybe I would be able to do that for Julian Warneke someday. Maybe it would help.

Edward pulled himself together. "You always make me feel so guilty. But it's not my fault. It's not my fault! I was trying to protect Chris. I really did try. Oh, Chris. Chris, I really did try."

A moment of silence. I wondered if he'd hung up.

"What else could I do? She shows up on my doorstep, I can't turn her away. She doesn't tell me she's seen Rugieri. Gone to his hearing, like he's not going to recognize her. Shit, of course he's going to recognize her—of course he's going to look for her. As soon as he knows she's in the Bay Area, he's going to look for her. He's going to look for me as a way to find her. He comes here and kills her dog first so he can get to her. I'm halfway to the vet's and then it hits me what she said. That she's gone and seen Rugieri. Rugieri— God, it's so crazy I don't even hear it when she tells me. I hear it like ten minutes later. I got her away from here so fast—"

"I thought Rugieri was in jail."

"Bullshit. Cops rousted him out of his hotel this morning for questioning."

I didn't reply. I looked out the window at the night view of drunks staggering under streetlights, cars zipping around double-parked buses, offices glowing, figures silhouetted. Business, bustle, all seen from my point of view, way up here. Politics, work. All me me me, how does it affect me.

"She should have been safe at Delacort's. I don't see how they connected me to Delacort. Oh, God—if I'd known, I never would have taken her back up to his house. Never." He was sobbing now, choking on regrets. "Oh, Chris, I'm so sorry."

I hung up, seeing her shadow-bathed face as she praised Edward, asserting her absolute trust in him.

Let him mourn.

If I'd hung up sooner, I might have heard the shuffle of footsteps in the inner corridor. As it was, I heard the faint creak of a door opening.

A door opening. I jumped out of my chair, hitting the light switch in the same motion. The office went dark, lighted only by streetlamps far below.

I crossed to the bookcase, not wanting to stand out against the pale window.

A figure slid into the room. It lingered near the door. Looking for a light switch? Coming from the lighted corridor, eyes not accustomed to the dark; looking for the switch in a room he'd never visited at night?

All the way across town I'd wondered why. Why had he come to my apartment with a phony client list? Why had he attributed to a client deductions only he could have made? (And I'd been the one to tell him why Judge Shanna disqualified himself. I'd tipped the first domino. My God.)

What would Harry Prough have done to me if I'd let him into my apartment? What would he do to me now?

My feet found the bottom shelf of the built-in bookcase. I felt myself climb, rising half a foot from the floor, pushing the books back, balancing needlessly on six inches of sturdy oak. My arms spread, my fingers touched worn spines. I could smell the dust of cracked bindings, the acid of yellowing paper.

I was flattened against the bookcase. Balanced just so.

Just so. Just like that night outside Julian Warneke's window. Just like my dream, except that there was no place to jump, no way to cut the cord of unacceptable reality.

Balanced on the bookcase as if release from fear were still an option.

But it wasn't.

I stood there and knew it, suddenly and finally. Suddenly and finally, I accepted—and rejected—my naked escapism.

I'd closed myself off from making friends. Shut myself away from my parents. Buried my grief.

Let myself languish on the ledge. Waiting for what? Rescue? Don Surgelato to ride up on his white horse and sweep me away?

Don Surgelato with a wife to whom he was newly committed?

Now, as ever, there would be no rescue. Only the things I'd fled therapy to avoid. I had no choice but to do what I'd done in Julian Warneke's office. I had no choice but to creep back inside. And this time, I would have to face—not merely see—what was in there.

I stepped off the bookshelf as the light came on.

Harry Prough and I blinked at each other.

He was unshaven and rumpled. Maybe hadn't been home since Rondi rescinded the contempt order. From across the tiny room, I fancied I could smell the upstairs jail. Bad plumbing, disinfectant, cigarette smoke; it had a way of clinging to your clothes.

"I really admired you," I said. "You were so good."

"In the sense of clever? Or moral?" He wilted into a chair, my chair. At his feet he dropped a big square briefcase, the kind you carry law books in.

"Both, I guess."

"So where did it get me?" His face was painfully lined, puffy. "I wuz railroaded, as they say. Four years' hard time. Wrecked my health. Didn't do a damn thing for my disposition, either."

"That was a long time ago."

He shook his head. "That was yesterday. That was ten minutes ago."

"You killed Chris Rugieri?" I wanted him to say no. My tone all but begged for contradiction.

"I made a call, yeah. Someone used to be in Highway Sixty-one." The corners of his lips curled downward. He looked like a young boy about to cry. "You don't go putting your friends in jail. You don't do that to your friends."

"Her friends were going to burn a baby."

"That was just talk." He leaned forward, fiddling with the clasps of his square case.

"Of course they'd deny it, after the fact."

"Barry Kilmer, they cut him up so bad his fourth year in jail he went blind. Joe Nideka ended up killing someone in a prison gang—he'll never see daylight. They'll get Rugieri on the state charge. And the two on parole, they're being jerked around so bad—drug tests, on-the-job harassment, you name it—they'll be back inside within a year."

Back inside. It was my worst fear, too. I looked at Harry Prough's haggard face and I felt his horror.

"You didn't have to make that call. You knew they'd kill her. How did that change anything? How did that help those people?"

He swiveled the chair so that he looked out at the night sky. "It told them I was sorry. Sorry I didn't win the case. Sorry I didn't keep them out of jail. Sweet Christine was too credible up there, with her serious face and her good family background." He rubbed his eyes. "Damn her."

"Why are telling me this? Why did you come to my apartment?" Give me a phony client list? Lie to me about Rugieri being in jail? Hunt me down at work?

"Because you got it."

"Got what?"

"The whole thing. The way you looked at me in the elevator—told me I should be in jail. You knew. You figured it out. You knew it was me."

"No, I didn't!"

"Baloney. You didn't let me into your apartment. Told me straight out you didn't trust me. I thought maybe if I put Surgelato's name on the list you'd open the door—"

"Why?" My voice was tight, explosive. "Why his name?"

"Huh—you don't know? For a while you were the hottest fucking item in lefty lawyer circles. Your mother used to piss and moan about it—red-diaper baby falls for superpig." He pressed his chin into his neck, creating a beagle collar of wrinkles. His eyes, under lowered brows, were suddenly grudging, almost childishly so. "Anyway, the bottom line is I can't let you tell. I won't go back to jail."

"But you just went." I was grasping at straws; talking to delay. "You went voluntarily to discredit Rondi."

"To get an alibi."

Oh, Jesus. And I'd thought . . .

"One night," Prough continued, "that felt like being in hell ten years."

Yes, I knew that feeling.

"I won't turn you in," I said quietly. "I know about jail. I wouldn't send anyone there."

A faint smile. "You testified against a friend. In law school."

A "friend" who'd killed three other friends. I was afraid he'd remember that.

It seemed an excellent time to leave. But my body felt encased, torpid. Prickling cold. My lungs knotted, refusing to exhale.

I made my foot slide forward, the motion unfamiliar, almost glacial. I watched Prough hoist his briefcase to his lap. An internal voice said he had a weapon; guessed the security guard had waved him past the metal detector as he'd waved me past. Prough was a familiar face, too, a regular.

I did a slow-motion shuffle through the door. Beyond the receptionist's desk.

I could hear metal pieces click and lock. I tried to hurry, tried to muster some adrenaline. But Jesus. I was paralyzed, not prodded, by my panic.

I glanced at the two doors before me, one leading to the corridor, one to the judge's chambers. I couldn't even think fast. Which was closer?

I took a few more plodding steps. Knowing, as I heard metal against metal, that a weapon was being assembled.

Maybe dawdling was another way of jumping. Giving up. I trudged, trapped in a slow dream, my consciousness hurling itself toward a door my feet couldn't seem to reach.

Which door? Judge's office? Corridor?

I wondered if I should turn, see what Harry Prough was doing. Try to discuss things, perhaps. A saw-edge of dread cut the heart out of me: Don't look. Deny.

I watched my arm reach for the corridor door, and in a rush of motion I was across the room. I touched the knob, my fingers stung by static electricity.

And abruptly, the door was flung open, flung so that it struck me, sent me staggering sideways, trapping me between the knob and the wall.

I heard the shrill imperiousness of outrage: "And what possible explanation can there be for this, Mr. Prough?"

I slid down the wall. In a moment, I would hear bullets cut down Manolo M. Rondi, U.S. District Court judge.

"Well, Mr. Prough? You do know that it is illegal to have such a weapon in your possession?" A long second of silence. "If you think you can protect your clients by smuggling weapons out of—"

Oh, God, he couldn't kill Manolo Rondi. Couldn't *kill* him.

I kicked the door, slamming it into the old man, battering

a strangled cry from him. I crawled out from behind it, crawled toward him, flailing my arms to push him.

"I should have known!" Rondi cried. "Should have known you two were conspiring—"

The last word caught in his throat as I catapulted to my feet and barreled into him, knocking us both into the hall. Trying to save the stupid son of a bitch's life, in fact. More than I'd been competent to do for my own.

I scrambled to my feet, pulling him up, too. Gasped a warning that died in my throat when he swatted me—hard blows with a wizened fist—and began screeching for a guard.

But bless the old fascist, a guard did come. A security guard pushed through the door leading to the public corridor. He pulled me away from Rondi, shouting, "Hey, now! Hey, now, whatcha doing to the judge?"

Pinioned by the guard, the three of us sitting ducks, I thought I might throw up.

But Harry Prough didn't shoot. He walked right past us, ignoring Rondi's furious accusations. Walked past as I tried to loosen the guard's grip on me, tried to get the guard to follow him.

Harry Prough walked right out the door.

36

THEY ARRESTED TOM Rugieri. They haven't found the weapon, though—I'm not sure they can make the charges stick without it. And they found Harry Prough in a Tenderloin hotel a few blocks from the Federal Building. He'd injected himself with a megadose of cocaine. They don't think he was a user. They think it was suicide.''

"He didn't want to go back to jail," the therapist said.

I nodded, taking some comfort in the sight of him, with his sandy hair and his tortoiseshell glasses, his bulky sweater.

Something about his face—it invited trust. I'd shopped around, taken time to find someone who seemed smart, not corny.

"It's a lot to work on," he observed.

"I know."

My money wouldn't last long, but I could stretch it six months, anyway. Until I figured out a few things. Like whether I wanted to be a lawyer. How to make friends. What, if anything, I wanted to do—or could do—about the appalling state of the nation. (That one might take a little longer. But not necessarily with my therapist. Maybe with my parents.)

"Well, where would you like to begin?"

I sighed. "This morning I threw my pot off the Golden Gate Bridge."

EPILOGUE

I TAKE THE gun I find in my boy's cheap room and with it I go and kill the *puttana* who ruins him. Already his whole life he spends in jail because of her and this ruins my family. My daughter Irena she does become another wild *puttana* that I will not speak or let in my house with her boyfriend black like a lump of coal.

That lawyer Prough already I don't like him, the way he talks to the judge in court. I think the judge is right, send him to jail four years, huh. For lack of respect I have no sympathy. He calls my son in his cheap room and he says, her name now is Rita Delacort and she is married to a lawyer, a big shot. My son he could be a big shot if he doesn't marry her. Instead him she ruins and then with my whole family in *disgrazia* and me so that I don't even show my face in the street, she marries a big shot.

I take the gun—my son does not hide it well. The first day I am here to visit I find the floor is not right and under it I find the gun. I am not afraid. What is to be afraid now that this *puttana* she has ruined Tomasino and made my daughter crazy to go live with a black animal.

I take first a bus and then a taxi to the mountain house. I worry that my son will be there already in his car, but he only hears the name of the *puttana* and he does nothing. He says he kills her dog and beats her boyfriend and that is enough. Enough—huh! Two times I send men to beat the *puttana*, but my son he does not know this. He sits and drinks his whiskey only. It makes a man dead to be in *prigione*. I see the same thing when Gigetto comes back from *campo di concentramento* in Germania. For three years he is whipped and has only potatoes to eat because the Germans have no heart and are animals. My brother comes back and he is good for nothing, only to sit and drink *vino* like my son drinks whiskey.

After the war, I am the one who is strong to come to America and learn the language and try to make my children *somebody*.

And now I am the one who is strong and goes to the top of the mountain with the big gun in a sack. I wish only that I could hang her upside down *nuda* like they do Mussolini's *puttana*. I only wish I can make her suffer. For her, to die is not enough.

For years and years I cry, I do not show my face in the street and my handsome boy he lives his life in *prigione* and now is good only to sit and drink whiskey.

I am sorry only that it is so fast with the gun and that the *puttana* does not cry and suffer forever for her sins.

Exciting
MYSTERIES
With A Legal Twist
by
Lia Matera